# LONGSHOT IN MISSOURI

**A novel of an unsung Civil War freedom-loving**

**soldier and spy**

Keith R Baker

K and L Products Press

Ronan, Montana

Keith R. Baker/K and L Products Press
P.O. Box 114
Ronan, Montana, USA/59864
www.KeithRBaker.com

Publisher's Note: This is a work of fiction. Names, characters, places, and incidents are a product of the author's imagination. Locales and public names are sometimes used for atmospheric purposes. Any resemblance to actual people, living or dead, or to businesses, companies, events, institutions, or locales is completely coincidental.

Ordering Information:
Quantity sales. Special discounts are available on quantity purchases by corporations, associations, and others. For details, contact the "Special Sales Department" at the address above.

Longshot In Missouri / Keith R. Baker -- 2nd ed.
ISBN - 13: 978-1517128807

## Dedication

This book could be dedicated to my great-great-grandfather, Robert Forrester, whose real life was a catalyst in the formation of this tale. Also to his wife, Bridget Murphy Forrester, who endured much and suffered much and died young after giving her all to raise their children. I never met either of them, nor knew of their existence until 100 years after their passing.

As a direct descendant of these two persons, I would not be here to research and to write, had they not lived the lives they did. Their lives were hard and full of hardship, as were the lives of all those living in those years. It is encouraging to find oneself descended from such people.

More recently, the wife of the author, Leni Ferenc Baker, has had more to do with the endless correcting and encouragement needed for this work to come forth. Any remaining errors are not hers, but mine. She is an incredible help in all things. It is to her and her boundless love and support that this book is dedicated.

Thanks, dear!

# Table of Contents

Chapter 1 - Pink At Sunset ......................................... 1

Chapter 2 -The Home Front ................................... 21

Chapter 3 - Counting The Cost ............................... 37

Chapter 4 - Camp Douglas Prison ......................... 49

Chapter 5 - Joy Of Deliverance .............................. 61

Chapter 6 - St. Louis Knights ................................. 73

Chapter 7 - Chicago Conflicts ............................. 103

Chapter 8 - Kentucky Bound ............................... 125

Chapter 9 - Richmond And Big Hill ..................... 139

Chapter 10 - On To Pleasant Hill ......................... 167

Chapter 11 - Leaving Kentucky ........................... 191

Chapter 12 - Planning Ahead ...............................201

End Notes ............................................................221

CHAPTER ONE

# Pink At Sunset

*Early Spring, April 3rd, 1862*
*After breakfast a few miles northwest of New Madrid, Missouri,*
*on a slight ridge overlooking a ford of St. John's Bayou*

Longshot eased his shoulders back while watching intently over the front sight of his long-barreled rifle. His eyes were focused in the distance. The gun's recoil was recently passed, yet only faintly noticed. He was aware of the small curl of smoke ebbing from the muzzle of the custom Sharps rifle. He also noticed the pinch in his nose from the burnt powder. He always did.

Nearly a half-mile distant from his hidden position, a uniformed rider turned in his saddle seeking the source of the shot's report reaching his ears, just in time to present his head and torso directly toward the oncoming projectile. It entered neatly through the man's chest, passing through and crushing his spine. He was dead instantly. At least Longshot hoped that was the case.

He didn't much mind his nickname; he'd had it since Camp Randall the previous year. His eyesight had so often been compared to others that he knew for fact his vision was extraordinarily keen. From experience with the Army, he knew his marksmanship skills to be superior to those of his fellow men. These facts set him apart, made him unique. They inspired his nickname.

This Confederate colonel and his artillery command had been instrumental in holding off advances against New Madrid by the Union Cavalry and infantry, using their well-aimed and well-practiced strategies and tactics in the field. The Army's commanding generals had given the order, which passed through the agency on to Longshot to complete. It was believed that killing this colonel would discourage the entire artillery unit and allow the Union forces to advance. Rob didn't know if that would happen or not. He'd done the job he was assigned, assassinated another human being for the cause of this war.

Coming back to the present moment, he noted the Confederate colonel's small contingent gathering excitedly around the body of their fallen leader. The lean, hawk-faced officer among them, who Rob recognized as the major who was second-in-command, pointed to the line of trees on the ridge which currently served as his concealment. The line being pointed out was off; his hiding place was much further west. Still, it was near enough to his position that he needed to make a hasty departure.

As part of his planning and preparation for carrying out this assassination he had already searched out not just one, but two escape routes down the rear slope of the ridge. He quickly loaded his gear and mounted his horse. Guiding the animal gently to the path that would lead him farthest from his pursuers, he fought the instinct to gallop down the farm road. Instead, he walked the horse down the forested slope about fifteen yards below that trail. The ground was mostly well-packed and only slightly damp. A few shallow depressions held enough moisture to be muddy, so he avoided those. He counted on making little or no noise and leaving almost no tracks. That was always part of his planning.

He was deeply into the wooded tract already, almost three-quarters of a mile away from his hiding spot, when he heard the sounds of a cavalry troop galloping in pursuit. Unfortunately for them, they had gone north and east, whereas his course was mostly west. The sounds of their headlong pursuit in the wrong direction soon faded from his ears. Much later he reined his horse more to the north, toward his intended meeting place.

Robert Finn was a farmer from the tiny town of Darien in southern Wisconsin. He had left his native Ireland during the height of the infamous Potato Famine there, and settled first in northern Illinois in 1847, later moving to Darien in 1852 with his new bride, Bridget.

He reflected on the complex and amazing twists of fate as he rode along toward his meeting with Allan Pinkerton. They had first met while Rob was working at a brewery in Dundee, Illinois over a dozen years earlier. The now-famous detective had not yet begun his agency in those years. He had been involved in the business of supplying beer barrels assembled by his coopers for the brewery to fill.

Pinkerton had been impressed by Rob's size and strength and had logged a mental note of those traits. "Pink", as a very few close friends called him to his face, was known for his remarkable ability to accurately assess the measure of a man and recall such details when the need arose. His employees and casual friends often called him Pink behind his back.

Rob owed a lot to Pinkerton: besides his nickname, Pink had given him the custom-crafted rifle he now carried; had arranged Rob's special position with the Northern Army; set up a lucrative compensation scheme and provided him the special documents he carried giving him the freedom and flexibility to carry out his orders. Those papers were signed by the President of the United States of America, one Abraham Lincoln. Lincoln himself had handed the warrants to Rob during a clandestine meeting at the Union League Club in Chicago which had, of course, been arranged by Pink.

Thus it was with a certain pride of accomplishment that Rob looked forward to this meeting. Pink was always generous with his compliments for successful missions and prompt to pay according to whatever agreement was in effect. His Colt Pocket

Revolver shifted in his tunic, again reminding him of the recent use of its deadly force during a mission that nearly went wrong. And that recollection teased the nagging element of his conscience into renewed activity. Was the assassination of wartime enemies really any different from any other type of murder?

He hated these kinds of thoughts, which at times plagued and haunted him. The war surrounding him was second only to that within. His moral compass was askew. How could the type of killing he was doing be acceptable in the sight of God and the Church? And yet, could it be wrong with the President and so many of his neighbors supporting the effort to end the South's succession from the Union?

He was further bothered by the fact that his friends and family did not know what he truly did for the Union Army. He wore a uniform bearing sergeant's chevrons and rode Army-issued horses. He received payments (through a secret fund) from the Paymaster of the US Army. He pretended to be a special courier operating on special orders from high echelons of the Army. This cover was not entirely false, he was on special orders. And at times he even carried messages between Pinkerton and Army officers or other agents.

While Bridget knew that he killed enemy soldiers, she had no idea the circumstances nor the number that had fallen to his long-range skill. He cringed at what she and others would think, should the full extent of his activities ever become known to them.

His preoccupation ceased abruptly when his mount stumbled slightly over a fallen log. It was mostly hidden by brushy growth and low light beneath the canopy of trees already starting to leaf out. Rob urged the horse on, his need to report on time fueling his actions now that he was again fully attending to the tasks before him.

In addition to a pay envelope that Pink would hand over, Rob had high hopes for any news from home. His last two letters from Darien had been worrisome, recounting the illnesses of one of the twins and also six-year-old Michael. Mention of a cholera outbreak in the environs of that small community had set fearful imaginings to work in his mind.

They were traveling at a moderate lope now that the terrain had leveled some. This was a pace that the horse should be able to keep without becoming winded, and yet ate up the miles rapidly. The early evening was pleasant enough for this time of year though the air would rapidly cool as the sun sank lower in the sky.

Relatively certain that the remaining ride would be uneventful, Rob turned his thoughts again to personal matters. What if one of the youngsters were to worsen and die? Did Bridget have enough help on the farm? What of her health? She'd been frail ever since giving birth to the twins in 1859. Was the neighbor girl Margaret McDonald really enough help to keep things running smoothly?

These and other thoughts swirled through his head until he found himself coming over a small rise and spotting the party of three men gathered around an expensive coach hitched to a team of four horses. The pond beside where the rig was parked had been their agreed-to meeting point. Pink was easily distinguishable even at this distance. He had a heavy dark beard, dark bowler hat, and elaborate shirt and tie worn with his medium weight frock coat, also of dark color. The man always dressed well and completely; he would be thus attired even in the warmer months ahead.

As Rob reined the horse to a halt alongside the small gathering of detectives, Pinkerton hailed him in his Scottish accented speech with, "What news, Longshot? May it be a good report yer bearing?"

"I'm hopin' y'll be happy enough t' hear it, sir," was Rob's reply, his speech accented by that lilt peculiar to natives of the Emerald Isle. His smile was genuine, if somewhat slightly suppressed by his own recent thoughts about his part in the mortality of others.

"Let's have it then, starting with accuracy of our information on the colonel," Pinkerton said, while moving to a small folding table with two folding chairs positioned so the men could discuss their business privately. "I always want ta know how our other agents' work helps or hinders those in your particular vocation."

"Sure an' it made my shadowin' of the man easier that I found him my very first night in the town. Thanks t' the descriptions o' the colonel an' his sidekick major, an' their love of gambling, it was nothing at all t' follow 'em for a couple of days until the pattern was fixed. Then when they took t' wearin' their uniforms again a blind man couldn't miss 'em. O' course, it helped being as I was in civilian clothes most o' the time myself," Rob explained. "Those files ya gave me were correct in every detail. All I had t' do, was get close an' keep shadowin' 'em for the best time an' place. Then plannin' my hide an' escape so's t' let the rifle do what she does best.

"They left the hotel right on time this mornin' followin' their regular route. As always, they stopped at the ford t' water their horses an' have a stretch. 'Twas done with one shot of a thousand yards, give or take. I rode here straight from where I saw him downed. I wasn't followed; even backtracked three times today t' make sure of it." His voice trailed off as he finished his report.

Pinkerton looked carefully at him and asked, "What time was he dealt the blow?"

"Had t' be after half-past nine this mornin'," said Rob after thinking a moment about it. "Maybe closer t' ten. I didn't have a chance t' check the time 'til I was well away."

Pinkerton looked at Rob studiously for a minute longer before reaching into his coat pocket to extract a pair of envelopes. "There's a little extra for being afield the additional two weeks. This other is yer mail from Darien–came ta the office just as we were leaving," Pinkerton said as he handed them over to Rob. "May the news from home be good also."

Rob had to fight the urge to snap the envelopes out of his employer's hand. He nodded when reaching carefully for the offered packets while saying, "Thanks, Mr. Pinkerton. You're too good t' us." He ripped open the letter from home before checking his pay envelope–he knew Pinkerton would not shortchange him.

"Good agents are worth taking care of, Longshot. You've served me well once again." He ended his words abruptly, having noticed a pained look crossing the big Irishman's face. "What is it, Rob?" using his subordinate's given name out of courtesy and concern. "Anything I can do?"

Rob's head was down, his shoulders had also slumped down. He looked as though he'd just received a physical beating. Slowly his head came up, tears welling the corners of his eyes. He tried to speak, couldn't. Instead he paused and sucked in a deep breath. He shook his head, then leapt to his feet, threw his head back and let out such a loud, mournful groan that it brought the other members of Pinkerton's traveling party from around the opposite side of the coach.

Tossing the open letter and pay envelope at the table, he rushed off to the edge of the pond and fell to his knees. He rocked back and forth for several minutes muttering to himself between sobs, "Why, oh why, God? Why the little ones?" The sadness in his tone and radiating from his entire being was almost tangible to the observers. To their credit they showed the good sense and respect of leaving him alone in his grief.

Pinkerton spoke quietly to his other men and the three of them withdrew a ways across the clearing while unobtrusively carrying a few folding chairs and the small camp table. All was accomplished with respectful decorum to allow their grieving acquaintance some private space.

Sometime later that evening, well after darkness had fallen, the fire had been made, a stew prepared and shared, Pinkerton sat with a cup of steaming coffee around the fire with his two detectives. They were idly discussing other mission plans— part of their current business. Rob stumbled, though lightly enough, on a large branch that had been unseen in the darkness. The three men, calmly yet expectantly, turned to see what their companion would do next.

Rob walked carefully to an open seat which had been thoughtfully placed in the circle around the fire pit. He carefully lowered his large frame to the chair and settled. Though his head was still down and his eyes seemed puffy in the firelight, his breathing was steady and regular. With a physical effort he gathered himself, shook his head and turned to face Pinkerton. He took a deep breath.

His voice began with a moan and cracked as he said between gasps, "Mr. Pinkerton, my boys Michael and Henry are gone ... Taken by the cholera ... an' now Bridget's got the ..." before he could finish, Rob's shoulders heaved and he put his hand to his face. His whole body was wracked with the emotional pain he was experiencing and it was difficult for the others to watch. "What am I gonna do, now, sir?" He fairly pleaded before again being beset by sobs. He repeated to himself, "What'll we do now?" many times over as he wrapped his arms about his own shoulders, put his head down and rocked disconsolately from side-to-side in his chair.

This sad scene went on for a while longer, Rob occasionally being calm enough to speak as well as to listen. Over the next hour or so Pinkerton soothingly assured him that he would be able to return home and attend to pressing family matters that had been revealed in the letter.

"Don't give it another thought, Rob. You'll go–leave tonight if ya want; though I think it would be wiser ta stay the night here with us and set out in the morning with me. Whatever you need. Take a couple of weeks. Make it a month. See me personally in the Chicago office when yer ready for another assignment. Don't worry another moment, lad. Things will be arranged. I'll wire instructions ta the staff tomorrow when we get into town."

Other than nodding his head in acknowledgement, Rob was unable to respond. Physical and emotional exhaustion kept him from even trying. The others set about the chores of straightening the campsite before turning in.  Rob was nowhere to be seen, but they were relatively unconcerned, since all the saddles and horses were accounted for.

Dawn found Rob tending a newly-made fire with the strong, pungent aroma of coffee mingling with the steam that vigorously escaped from the tin pot on the portable grating over the fire. He was the first to call out in greeting, "Good mornin'," to each of the others as they approached the fire area after attending to their morning toilet routines.  As the last man arrived to take his place around the fire, he saw that Rob was removing the fried bacon to a warming plate that was placed solidly on a large, flat rock near the coals. He sounded nearly cheery when he asked the group, "Hope ya don't mind the eggs scrambled? Only way I know t' make 'em."

Following a general murmur of agreement and head-nodding, Pinkerton asked at large, "Everyone get a good rest, then?"  Again there came mumbled assent and nodding, to which Rob added, "I moved a ways off so's you'd not be kept awake by my snores."

"We need ta get to St. Louis as soon as possible. Longshot, do ya know if this town of Bloomfield has a telegraph office?"

"It does indeed, sir. An' if it happens not t' be workin' there's another one in Sikeston beyond." Rob's response took into account the frequent breaks in telegraph service owing to intentional sabotage far more often than weather or equipment-related failures.

"Good enough. After we send the wire, we'll be taking the train to St. Louis and then Chicago. Should cut a couple days off the travel. I'll see ya home as fast as can be, Rob."

A simple nod was his only reply; the only one needed in these sad circumstances.

The men hurriedly finished their breakfasts and cleaned up the camp area. Rob and Pinkerton were happy to get away on horseback while the other two finished the chores. Though brisk, the air was not so cold as what they could expect upon returning to northern Illinois and southern Wisconsin.

The Bloomfield telegraph office was closed, but the stop at the telegraph office in Sikeston was brief and successful. While there, they learned of a passenger train that they could easily catch if they hurried. Horses and saddles were left at a local livery operation that had a contract with the Federal government. They found the station, and ticketing and boarding all went smoothly. The rest of the trip northward to St. Louis was uneventful, for which both men were grateful. Both had plenty to think about and the hours passed mostly in silence between them because of it.

Rob shared more of what detail he'd had from the letter. His oldest child, Catherine–Cath, as she preferred to be called– had started the letter and then the young neighbor woman, Margaret McDonald, had taken it up. It was brief–there was not much to tell. Henry, one of the two-and-half-year-old twins, had succumbed to the dreadful disease. He was followed two days later by his six-year-old brother, Michael. Rob's wife now had the initial symptoms. The only good news in the letter was that none of the other children were reported sick.

Allan Pinkerton was no stranger to death and its after-math, having been a close observer of it so frequently due to his business. He knew that they were racing against an unstoppable clock for his employee to arrive before the youngsters' burials. Given the time it had taken for the message to reach Rob, his arrival was almost certain to be too late. Despite a best effort for speedy travel, it seemed unavoidable. Communities wanted, even demanded that the bodies be put in the ground quickly when cholera was the agent of death. As for the man's wife, Pinkerton knew well the terrible odds against a person of her frailty once the disease was upon them. He wisely and graciously kept these thoughts to himself. Sharing them would do nothing good.

He'd had several things to consider choosing to route through St. Louis instead of taking the slightly more direct, thus possibly faster one passing through Cairo, Illinois. The first and most important of those being keeping Longshot's cover intact. There was no way of knowing whether someone from either side of the river, or the war, might recognize him from his surveillance activities during the preceding weeks. Then there was that other business in St. Louis, which was for the time being, at least, more of a personal, private matter. No sense taking chances with Finn's safety, he'd finally decided. They would be better off going through St. Louis. That's what he told himself, anyway.

They dined well in St. Louis where Pinkerton arranged and paid for two separate rooms in the lower floors of the famous Planters Hotel. He settled the dinner bill and gratuity before leaving Rob alone to finish his dinner and linger over his coffee. He explained his departure by saying that he had a small matter to attend to and that he would see Rob over breakfast at 7:00 the next morning. Finn's look of surprise was fleeting and he soon returned to his introspective regarding his family situation.

Once outside, Pinkerton stepped off at a brisk pace along Fourth Street and quickly reached Pine. Since he knew his course precisely, there was no hesitation choosing which way to turn as he purposefully strode along. His intended destination was not far ahead.

Though it was late, a lamp yet burned within the spaces of the street-level office. Pinkerton employed his own shadowy tactics of remaining hidden while watching through the main window for signs of human activity. He was soon rewarded when an aged, hunched form passed from the rear office to the front area seeking after something on a desk there. The man returned to the rear office after just a few moments, search, clutching a sheaf of papers in his right hand.

Pinkerton quickly and quietly slipped the specially-crafted tool he carried for just this purpose between the door and the jamb. With a few slight, deft movements of his hand the door was unlocked and opened silently on its hinges. He moved stealthily into the space and secured the door behind himself. Then he passed to the open entry of the rear office without a sound. The elderly man behind the desk was seated and so bent over his work that the only view of him presenting itself was of a thick, bushy head of white hair.

He called out using a calm and quiet tone, "Theo, do not be alarmed. It's me, Allan." Though obviously startled, the older man was fully in control of his emotions when he answered, "And still sneaking up on honest men trying to do a day's work, I notice." His small smile grew to light up his whole face. He then rose from the desk chair where he'd been seated to work, crossing quickly to the newcomer in his presence. "Always good to see you, Allan, despite your rascally ways."

"And likewise to ya', Theo, likewise. I got your message a little while back but couldn't come 'round in person until now. Does the matter of the KGC still need the help of my crew? Do we still have time t' do any good?"

Seating himself back down behind the desk, the aged proprietor gestured for Pinkerton to do likewise in a chair arranged to allow for close, private conversation. He thought for a moment or two, then replied.

"As it turns out, timing couldn't be better even if you and I had planned it out. They're meeting regular now and not just in Jacksonville and St. Louis. The Order has Temples in just about every city and town both sides of the river. They seem to be well-funded and organized. I think that right now is the time to introduce your infiltrators during this mad rush of their growth. What happened with Fort Henry and Fort Donelson seemed to get 'em all whipped up. This battle for Island No. 10 and all the troops moving south are bringin' their blood up. Should be an easy matter to get them in, find out their plans and get out."

This man, Theobald Forrester, was a Scottish-born immigrant, the same as Pinkerton. Old enough to be Allan's father, he had been a friend of the Pinkerton family before either he or Pinkerton left Scotland. He was an accomplished accountant and bookkeeper whose services were sought out by the wealthy and successful folks of St. Louis, who had learned to trust the old Scot's honesty, integrity and tight-lipped way of doing business.

By pretending to despise the Federal government's practices relative to permits, licenses and control with some of his clients, he had managed to gain the confidence of several among the more radical of such thinkers. He kept a very low profile and most of his customers merely knew him as hardworking, honest and loyal in his business dealings.

Though Forrester had been successful in these ruses thus far, he could ill-afford to be found out for his real sympathies without grave danger to himself and his family. Being caught meeting privately with Pinkerton in his office at night could easily result in harm to them all. Both men were well aware of those risks. Both believed that dissolving the Union of their adopted country was the worst thing imaginable and were prepared to do whatever they could to avert it.

Despite Forrester's encouraging words to the contrary, effectively infiltrating the Knights of the Golden Circle would never be an easy task, nor one without danger of making a full sacrifice for one's beliefs. The Knights, or KGC, or the Order, as it was variously known, was not made up of trifling men. The Oath of the Order was brutal in its demands for retribution against those who opposed them. One line of that Oath contained the following: "I do furthermore swear to bear hatred, that nothing but blood shall satisfy, against all men of the North who are not friendly to our cause." It was a lengthy oath promising to "sow seeds of hatred and revenge" and more. Its designers and adherents were fully committed to all-out elimination of their enemies. Once inside the organization, there would be no easy escape from it.

The two men continued their talk a short while longer, both being aware of the danger of drawing attention to Pinkerton's visit. After exchanging additional details of locations, times, and names of prominent persons involved, the old bookkeeper moved to his safe, worked the combination and removed a single sheet of paper, which he handed over to his younger friend. "And it may be that the hopes of the Union ride upon the work of you and your men, Allan. Godspeed." Though weary, he smiled through hopeful eyes as he passed it to Pinkerton.

"On my way at once," the detective announced as he rose to leave, straightening his coat and tie. He retrieved his hat from the wall peg where he had placed it before sitting down just a short time earlier. "I'll be in touch if I need anything else, and ya' know how t' reach me." Theo accompanied him to the front door where they shook hands. Then he opened the door, and checking his surroundings, Pinkerton stepped outside and was immediately swallowed up by the darkness. Carefully closing the door after his guest Theo breathed, "And may God deliver you and all of us from the hotheads in this land, Allan." Forrester's comment was uttered to the empty room in which he stood.

Upon his return to the hotel, Pinkerton retrieved his keys from the front desk along with his messages, of which there were two. One was from his Chicago office confirming the details of travel and other arrangements he had asked to be made. The other was a telegram from Washington in reply to one he had sent earlier in the day. Its short message, though expected, sent a small shiver through the North's spy master. "Proceed with all haste and abandon. Funding authorized. Signed, A.L."

Allan Pinkerton had just been given the go-ahead order by the President of the United States for what would possibly turn out to be the most dangerous mission and assignment of his career to date. He wondered how costly it would be for the men who would carry it out. And though he knew it to be unlikely, he dared to hope that none of them would be killed or injured. He had his reasons for being distant with his men. Letting himself form friendships was not an option. With that thought in mind, he was a little concerned about his attachment to Rob Finn, the man he had recruited to his service and nicknamed Longshot. The man who was suffering great distress over the death of two of his young children and the dangerous illness now attacking his wife. Would the man be up to the task Pinkerton had in mind? Hard to know. And nothing could be decided until the poor fellow had at least had the chance to bury his dead and make what arrangements he could for his surviving family's comfort and sustenance.

CHAPTER TWO

# The Home Front

*April 11th, 1862*
*The train station in Darien, Wisconsin*

The Racine & Mississippi Railroad train that had delivered
Rob to his hometown the day before, was now returning to its
home station in Racine after an overnight passage out to Free-
port, Illinois.  Slowing as it pulled into the little station, the whistle blew, and the wind-driven sleet beneath the scudding gray
clouds did nothing to lift anyone's spirits.  Right now, Rob's spirits could have used some uplifting.  He had never felt so lost, so
low and so alone in all his life.  Leaving his parents, siblings,
cousins and friends behind when he left Ireland had been nothing
by comparison.

At forty-two-years-old, he arrived home in time to learn
that both his dead sons had been removed and buried by the
county authorities; that his thirty-two-year-old emotionally dis-
traught and physically ill wife had died only hours before his arrival and her body, shrouded against contagion and lying within
the plain pine coffin at the end of the siding, would be under-

ground in a matter of hours. No one in the family yet knew for certain where the boys had been buried. The health commission had handled that matter in haste and without regard for family feelings.

Their travel between St. Louis and Chicago had been interrupted several times by troop movements being hurriedly shuffled southward–too late to be engaged in what was called the Battle of Shiloh Church in Tennessee. By all accounts it had been the bloodiest engagement yet. Starting with their riverboat crossing at St. Louis and then the train up to Alton and on into Chicago, Allan Pinkerton and Rob Finn had only been able to watch for several hours on each of five different occasions while their train was side-tracked. The trip, which normally took less than twenty-four hours, lasted three days.

Today he would accompany Bridget's remains to Elkhorn where the county's health commissioners promised that she would be buried in the Roman Catholic section of the big cemetery there. The cholera epidemic sweeping through the area had taken its toll in human life and suffering; the toll upon county resources was no exception. The numbness he felt as the cold, wet wind beat at his exposed skin was a reflection of the numbness he carried in his heart and mind. He did not care. He could not imagine how he would go on living. He forced himself to think of his remaining four children who were now motherless, and wondered how he would be able to take care of them with

Bridget gone. He couldn't go back to his position with the Union Army and the Pinkerton Agency–that was plainly unthinkable. For a brief moment that thought bolstered him as he realized he'd no longer be ordered to kill other men.

His misery returned as a familiar coach-and-four pulled to a stop, and Allan Pinkerton alighted from the passenger compartment. Pinkerton glanced around, quickly assessed the circumstances by the appearance of the simple coffin and the look on Rob's face. He then extended his hand in a firm greeting, but with no mirth or joy mixed in. "Oh, Rob! I am so, so sorry for yer loss," he said as he gently gripped the grieving man's right hand in his own. He brought his left hand up and placed it on Rob's shoulder. The greater height of the new widower made the gesture somewhat unnatural and uncomfortable, neither of which detracted from the sincerity which accompanied it. "When did she pass?"

"'Twas yesterday mornin', just a couple hours before my train got in," he said in a surprisingly controlled and even voice. The simple fact was that he was all cried out. He had no more tears just now for anyone nor anything. The numbness he was experiencing in his mind and spirit made him think he might never care enough to have tears again.

While Pinkerton had known with great likelihood that the man's wife would die, the fulfillment of that expectation did not diminish the genuine pain and sorrow he felt. He was not the unfeeling person others made him out to be. He merely hid his feelings from others and even from himself at times. He was aware of a deep sorrow growing within and ordered his mind to control his emotion. For just an instant, his resolve for his plan involving Finn wavered. That instant passed, however, and he took up his role as employer and comrade-in-arms again. "Let's see what needs to be done, shall we?" he asked while gently leading Rob by the elbow to duck into the coach and out of the weather. "Where are the other children now?"

"They're at the house with young Cath an' Maggie, sir," Rob replied, using the formal address customary in their business relationship. "I'm afraid I'll not be returnin' t' your service after all, though. Sorry t' disappoint ..." Rob's voice trailed off revealing uncertainty about his surroundings, his future, everything. He had been set adrift by the turn of events in his family over the past ten days. Three of the dearest people to him on the whole Earth, dead, and in under two weeks. Was this the wrath of God at work for what he had done in the field of "battle," he wondered?

Rob was not exactly a religious man. He believed in God and he respected the priests of the Church. He attended as regularly as possible without being harsh with himself when he couldn't. But much of what he practiced of the Catholic religion he did to make Bridget happy. Bridget was the religious one of the family. Or had been. Now she was dead. She'd never harmed anyone, was even opposed to Rob's going off to war. Why did she die? What had caused God to end her life instead of his? And what about the deaths of their two sons? What had they done to deserve early graves? Though he'd been pondering these same thoughts ever since receiving the news of the boys' deaths, there were no answers that worked. Would the righteous God that he had learned of from the Church punish him by killing his family members? He hoped not–it did not seem right to him. He could not fathom the whole mess.

Pinkerton merely blinked and nodded at Rob's last remark, then said, "Sure, sure, I know. There's no need ta talk of such things right now, is there, Rob? You've plenty ta manage for the time being." His calm demeanor and steady voice helped to calm Rob again, for which he was grateful. Not that Rob had expected an argument. It was just good to know that Mr. Pinkerton understood the difficult place he found himself in and wasn't going to try to talk him out of his plan to remain in Darien. Pinkerton was wise enough in the ways of the world to know that time was the great healer of wounds. And though his missions planned for Illinois, Missouri and Kentucky would not allow him to remain idle, he would allow as much time to pass as possible, in deference to the other's need. "No need ta worry about such things at all, Rob, not at all." This final reassurance had the effect of deepening Rob's gratefulness and appreciation at having such an understanding man as his former employer.

"Listen though. Is there anything, anything at all that ya' need or that I can do ta help see ya' through this difficult time? Money isn't everything, I know, but it can help ease some of life's burdens. How about I just spot ya' fifty dollars ta help tide ya' over. No need ta pay it back until yer back on yer feet. No hurry whatever."

Rob's mind was reeling at the generosity of the offer. He suddenly had a number of expenses attached to the recent illnesses and deaths. Fifty dollars was enough to help him into the fall of the year, when his harvest came in and he could pay it back with money left over for the winter. His hope rose slightly. He reckoned that maybe, in all his current darkness, there really was cause for hope. Could Pinkerton be some sort of angel? He was certain that Bridget would have thought so. An odd notion, he thought. The few times she had met Pink, she later told Rob that he made her nervous. Imagine that! An angel making St. Bridget nervous.

He realized that he was smiling weakly at the memory of the teasing nickname that he had given her for devoutly observing her religious beliefs. It had been done in fun and in love. Now she was gone ... the smile disappeared from his face.

"Sir, that's too much money. It would take a poor farmer like me forever t' repay that much. I do appreciate yer kind offer." He looked aside knowing that his eyes would well-up with the emotions he was now feeling.

"Rob, my good man. Take it. If ya' don't need it, don't spend it. Better ta have it and not need it than ta need it and not have it. As I said, no rush to pay me back. Actually it's the agency's money and the agency is flush just now." He winked a friendly smile of assurance at Rob, who surrendered the argument.

Again experiencing the emotional wave when touched by another's generosity, Rob swallowed hard before looking down at the coins that had been placed in his hand. "I won't forget this, sir, ever. An' I'll be payin' it back before ya' know it. Ya' can count on me, sir."

To himself Pinkerton thought, "And I will be counting on ya', Rob, even though I wish I didn't have ta. Yer chance ta pay back the debt will come soon enough, friend. Plenty soon enough." Instead of speaking these thoughts, he just looked at the big man's face, shook his hand again, and smiled. Then he added, "Rob, I wish I could stay longer, especially under these circumstances. But duty calls; I must away. I hope ya' understand."

"I do, sir. I really do. An' thank ya' fer yer generous loan o' th' gold. Ya' won't be sorry. I'll see t' that."

Again Pinkerton's thoughts echoed only to himself, "I won't be sorry no matter how things turn out. I just hope ya' won't end up in a sorry state, either." As Rob was exiting the coach, Pinkerton nodded to the driver, signaling their departure from the dreary little town where he had just cast a net of control over someone he genuinely respected and liked. The twinge of guilt passed quickly, however. Such things almost always did.

Skillfully applying his coachwhip to get the horses' attention, the driver turned the conveyance completely about and drove them out of town in the direction from which they'd come. Pinkerton would be back into Illinois within the hour and in Chicago before the day was out.

* * * *

*After breakfast, Sunday, May 26th, 1862*
*The Finn family home in Darien, Wisconsin*

Big and strong a man though he was, Rob was not handling his losses well. It had been over six weeks since he had buried Bridget and since he last had seen his former employer, Allan Pinkerton. His lethargy was palpable enough to cause his children and their nanny, Maggie, to notice and worry about his lack of interest in daily matters. His eldest child, Cath, who was exceptionally mature for one so young was not worried about him. She was not yet thirteen years old. And she was angry with her father. Her anger was thinly being held in check. There were none of the usual smiles and laughter that had been her trademark behaviors in days past, before her father had, "gone off t' his silly war," as she often put it.

Her dam of resolve which had been holding back her emotion burst completely late that Sunday morning. Cath and Maggie were struggling to get the younger children fed and dressed in time to attend the Mass being held in Potter's Barn on the edge of the nearby town of Delavan. The parish priest from the Lake Geneva Church held these traveling sacraments only once each month and the family had missed the last one due to the two boys' passing and their mother's illness at that time. Cath favored her late mother's devout religious practice and felt strongly that the other children needed what comfort their religious faith could offer. She further did not deny her own need for such. And yet there sat her father, whom she loved and adored her entire life, his arms folded on the table and his head atop his arms. He appeared to be snoozing. Bad enough that he had already announced his own non-attendance, but he did not so much as lift a finger to help ready the youngsters. She'd had more of his moping about than her courageous young soul could abide.

"An' will ya' still be sitting right there nursin' yer sorrows when we get back?" Her question was delivered at full-volume, flush- faced and with hands on her hips. Her defiant posture and attitude was accentuated by her red hair and intense green eyes. "I've had quite enough o' yer uselessness, Mr. Robert Finn, ya' great big oaf! Really I have! Help or get out o' th' way, at least, can't ya?"

Though born in Illinois and raised in southern Wisconsin, Cath had taken much of her Irish accent from her parents as well as their many Irish-born neighbors and friends. Immigrants tended to clan together in the communities where they lived, whether small rural towns or larger cities such as Milwaukee or Chicago. Her temperament was easy to spot as being Irish. Her initial outburst over, she resumed the tasks she'd been attending to before she spoke. She was like a diminutive whirlwind as she brushed her sister Mary's hair and turned to straighten the remaining twin's coat. As Cath went to retrieve her own worn coat and hat and herd the children out the door, Maggie, who was only seventeen years old, waded in to Rob's defense. She was also born in Ireland and well-enough able to hold her own against the likes of the younger girl. Or so she thought.

"Now just a minute, Missy! How dare you talk t' your own father that way? An' him being such a recent widower an' all. You mind your place an' your manners or... or there'll be trouble!" Maggie grew flushed with the emotion of the moment and glared at Cath.

"Trouble? Not from th' likes o' you goin' about makin' cow-eyes at me father while me own mother's not two months in th' grave. There'll be no trouble from th' likes o' you that I can't handle." Her retort surprised them all. Cath herself was even a little taken aback by it. The truth of her own words had not penetrated to the forefront of her thoughts until she had spoken them in this moment of duress. But once out, they could not be taken back–ever. An uncomfortable hush fell over them all.

Rob stood up to his full height, looked at the two contestants and surveyed his other children. Without another word he navigated around the table and out the back door, slamming it behind him.

Cath looked helplessly at Maggie and offered a deep shrugging sigh as she said, "I'm so sorry, Maggie. I never meant t' say those things. Really I didn't. I don't know where they came from, but I surely didn't mean them. Ya have t' believe me!"

Maggie knew that Cath had not intended to hurt her feelings, that she had just been upset by her father's behavior lately. That and the stress of the family preparing for Church had pushed the girl past the normal boundaries of propriety. Yet the truth of Cath's words stung more than a little. Maggie had been infatuated with Rob since they had first met a couple of years before. She knew it had been silly and improper all along but could not deny what the younger girl had seen. Nevertheless, she felt sorry for the tension she had contributed to the family that morning.

"There, there, Cath. We'll hear no more about it. Past an' forgotten. I didn't mean t' be sharp with you either. I hope you'll forgive me?" She had been tempted to pat the younger girl's hand but thought better of it. "We shouldn't fight each other, especially in front o' the children an' your father. I'm sure we can get along, can't we?"

Cath looked down and then away to where the others were gathered by the door waiting. She was aware of just the slightest hint of welling in the corners of her eyes that she did not wish for anyone to see. "Yes. We're fine. I really didn't mean t' cause trouble nor hard feelin's, Maggie." She took another deep breath to calm herself completely, then turned to the children who were already looking less concerned. "Let's go, children," she said, "we don't want t' keep the McSweeneys waitin'."

With that they were out the door heading east along the small main street of the town to where the wagon they would ride in was waiting. John McSweeney and his wife Mary were older than Rob and had a batch of their own children to haul around. They were familiar with the pain of loss, having had three children who were no longer above ground. They were especially patient with their own children as well as those from other families. Mrs. McSweeney jumped from the front seat of the aging wagon to help load the newcomers into the back for the ride to Delavan. If all went well, they just might get there before the service started.

"There you all are, looking smart an' clean as whistles," she said in a friendly and welcoming voice. "We can make it in time if we don't dawdle." With that she hoisted young Robert up to Maggie, who was already aboard, and helped Cath get John settled. With the last of the Finn family firmly in place, she returned to her seat beside her husband, who started the team by releasing the hand brake and giving the reins a light snap.

\* \* \*

Rob found himself sitting in what had recently become a favorite spot to think and ponder. He was under what was probably the largest oak tree on the land he farmed. Just at the far edge of the field adjoining his house, it was quiet and private, two things he had been valuing greatly in the weeks since Bridget's death.

He was disgusted with himself. Cath was right. He had been sulking and shirking his responsibilities to his family. That thought, in addition to ushering in a flood of guilt, made him sick in his stomach. This had to stop. And stop it would. Self-pity would solve nothing and it was wrong for him to expect his family to have to watch him wallow in it. They needed providing for, and he would step back into the harness to see that those needs were met. The moment that thought came into his head he knew it to be the right thing, the very thing he needed to grasp onto. There would be no more of this feeling sorry for himself. He would move forward.

Though he had adamantly told himself he would never return to the work he had been doing for Pink and the Union

Army, there was a notion in that direction that nagged at him. Yes, it had paid well. Yes, he was good at it, which he would have known even if Pink and others aware of his successful missions had not been so complimentary. He was an excellent long-distance shooter. He was a fierce fighter in close quarters, able to overpower and overcome most other men. He was very good at killing. He was, or had been, an assassin. He hated that word and the very thought of it. Even the idea of going back to it gave him a chill.

June would shortly be upon them. He had not fully prepared the soil of his fields for planting–his moping about had seen to that. He would need to hire help to plant and harvest a crop at all this season, and it would probably not be a good one. The loan of fifty dollars weighed heavily upon him, since he knew that a lean harvest would not produce sufficient cash to sustain the family and repay the loan. He started to consider the alternative of sharing-out his fields to his neighbors and returning to Pinkerton's employ. The prospect bothered him from the troubling moral aspect while giving him hope for an improved financial outcome. Not knowing which way he would choose, he decided to give it more thought.

Full of his new resolve to take charge of matters at home, Rob returned to the house and started cleaning and straightening; first the common areas of the house and then his own bedroom. For the first time he handled some of Bridget's personal things, putting them carefully into a basket. He was tempted to return to his brooding ways a couple of times but quickly put them aside. He would not let those around him down any longer. His strong will and determination would win out against the sorrow and depression he had been allowing to control his life and theirs.

He had drawn a bath, bathed, dried and changed into clean clothes and was arranging a few spring wildflowers he had picked on his way back from the oak tree. A pot of simple stew was simmering on the stove. Maggie had prepared it yesterday and it smelled wonderful. The front door opened slowly while Cath and the other children peered cautiously around it, followed by Maggie as they entered the house.

Rob's gentle spirit was such that he bore no anger nor upset toward Cath. She had been right, after all. Though her words had hurt, they had been true and heartfelt. And they had been deserved. He was a humble enough soul to recognize all this and to appreciate and love his daughter all the more for her frankness. She had managed to free him from his self-imposed prison of sorrow merely by pointing out his duty to his family. A little abruptly, perhaps ... but it never was easy being Irish, he thought to himself.

His smile revealed an array of feelings towards his family: his love, concern and desire for their well-being, all mixed with a touch of sheepishness regarding the way he had conducted himself for far too long. Looking out from under the wild shock of brown hair crowning his head, his hazel-grey eyes twinkled as they had not for some time. "Look who's here! If it isn't th' wee bairns an' their keepers," he enthusiastically referred to Maggie and Cath, who shepherded the others. Those two looked at each other with surprised smiles, having already taken in the change in the surroundings and improvement in Rob since they'd left earlier. Their delight in both was obvious.

"Something smells really good, Daddy," Mary said with youthful enthusiasm. "Are you making dinner?" Her emphasis on the last word of the question indicated her level of surprise. She was next oldest after Cath and so was more confident than her younger siblings.

"Maggie made it, I've just set it t' heatin'," was Rob's honest answer. "Not that I couldn't have whipped up a little somethin' if I'd a mind t'," he winked at Mary, and then turned his smile on Cath and Maggie, in that order. "An' which I have a mind t' presently, so's I'll be helpin' more with the chores again. That okay with you?" he asked to the family in general, his smile beaming into each face as he looked at them in turn.

Cath threw her arms around her father and hugged him close. "Oh, Daddy," she said several times, her joy at the return of the father she loved so well was obvious to them all.

CHAPTER THREE

# Counting The Cost

*Thursday, July 10,1862*
*Somewhere on the Chicago and Northwestern tracks north of Chicago*

While the train headed toward Chicago, Rob's thinking about his meeting with Allan Pinkerton had not changed much. Their series of telegraphed messages back and forth in the preceding twenty days had settled a few questions about his prospective return to the agency's workforce while raising a few more.

Yes. Pinkerton wanted him back and assured him that he would have an adequate salary to sustain his family.

No. He would not be going back to his earlier role of assassin with a long-range rifle.

More detail than that would have to wait until the men met in person. Rob was feeling better about returning to the detective agency once he learned he wouldn't merely be a hired gun. A phrase that Pinkerton had used in one of his brief telegrams had made him wonder what the current assignment, or series of assignments, might be. That phrase, "not without significant risk", was typical of communication with the nation's spy director. It contained truth without revealing any real description of what services he would be expected to give. Best to just wait for the meeting and not get himself worked up by speculations which would likely be wrong anyway.

During his stay in Darien, he had had time to reconnect with friends there who had helped him in the past and seemed intent on helping to make him whole again as he worked through his grief. Thomas Duffy and Robert Morris had both provided opportunities to help Rob earn money, as well as offering what they could in the way of caring for his children. In Thomas' case, that included allowing his own household helper, Margaret (Maggie) McDonald, stay on indefinitely at the Finn home to help manage. This arrangement had originally been offered as an inducement for Rob to "sign up and lead our town's lads aright" when he had enlisted the previous fall.

When the company had arrived at Camp Randall in Madison, Wisconsin, among other training disciplines they underwent target practice with the long-barreled .58 caliber Springfield muzzle-loading rifle. Rob's exceptional size and visual acuity had the training cadre wagging their heads in disbelief at his prowess. Some claimed never before to have seen such accuracy. Within days, word of Rob's uncanny marksmanship got out. In less time than he could have imagined possible, he was being interviewed by none other than his old acquaintance from his brewery days in Dundee, Allan Pinkerton.

Pinkerton also recalled that Rob, though not a brawler as such, was as tough as he was big when it came to a fist fight. The local toughs in Dundee avoided the big Irishman, as rumor got around that he could handle himself in a fight. The training sergeants at Camp Randall verified that Rob excelled during limited physical combat encounters offered to the new soldiers.

When Pinkerton offered him the special position, Rob hadn't really given a lot of thought to what his assignment as a "sharpshooter" might be like. The pay and other arrangements of the job were so far beyond anything he had imagined for himself that he accepted the offer almost without hesitation. He imagined that his calling would be to shoot advancing Confederate units on the field of battle. After all, all soldiers knew at some level that their job was to kill enemy soldiers. Not having to complete the basic training of marching, bayonet practice and the rest was a further inducement.

Once on the Pinkerton payroll, he learned that his expectations were not even close to those of his superiors. He was given  special training in the use of knives, pistols and other close-quarter fighting techniques. Because of his strength and speed, he excelled at these training sessions. The training was over quickly and his first assignments were following and surveilling individual "targets" right within Chicago itself. Some of those targets had been other Pinkerton agents whom he'd not yet met. Others were actual suspects of some sort, so their being chosen as targets to watch was real. Though he didn't know why they were being watched, it was obvious that the information being recorded on those men's activities, companions and whereabouts was the stuff that really made the agency run. His other surprise had come upon learning the names of two of those he had shadowed. Those two, in particular, were well-known businessmen in the Chicago community.

As the train approached the station in Chicago, Rob prepared to disembark the rocking conveyance with relief. Even the amount of time he'd spent riding the rails in previous months had not lessened his discomfort. He disliked being closed-in in the cars, the noise of the clacking wheels on the rails and the choking coal smoke that accumulated along the way. In short, he was no fan of travel by rail. He had to admit that the speed was unsurpassed on a long trip. He simply didn't like the confounded things much. The conductor called, "End of the line. Everybody off," bringing him back to the present. Disembarking quickly, he was soon walking the familiar environs nearing the Pinkerton's National Detective Agency's home office.

A small bell attached to the doorframe of the entryway to the main office jingled to announce his arrival. Several heads looked up from desks to see who it was that had entered their spaces. Two of them smiled recognition and welcome: Molly

Ferguson and Emmy Stewart. Both were attractive, pleasant young women of Scottish extraction. Both were good at their respective roles in the agency's office operations. After a brief but warm greeting during which the ladies extended their condolences to Rob, Molly cut to the matters at hand. "Mr. Pinkerton is expecting you, Rob, and I have orders to bring you in right away." Without further delay, she turned about and marched to the closed office door clearly labeled with the owner's name "Allan Pinkerton", on an impressive plaque. She knocked, paused, opened the door and announced, "He's here, Mr. Pinkerton." Turning to Rob she said, "Go right in, Rob. It's good to see you back."

Pinkerton was already halfway to the door with a hand extended in greeting. "Rob, my boy. So glad ya' could make it. It's good ta see ya'," then a brief pause followed by, " Yer looking well."

"Feeling more mysel' these days, thanks t' you in no small part, sir," Rob said. Pinkerton noted that the man was standing taller and appeared much more the man he had originally known and hired than the person he had last seen in the weather in Darien. "Let me take yer hat, lad. Have a seat." Pinkerton was adept at making people feel at ease in his presence.

Rob was again struck by the use of the term 'lad' that Pinkerton had applied to him. He knew they were only five or six years apart in age and Rob towered over the Scotsman. Pinkerton referred to everyone of the male gender as 'lad' and this was especially true when addressing his detectives and agents in private settings.

"I'll come straight at it, Rob. I not only want ya' back, ya'are really needed for this job." He paused while steadily surveying the other's eyes and face. Since Rob seemed relaxed, Pinkerton forged ahead. "Y've undoubtedly heard about the opening of Camp Douglas here in Chicago? An' yer probably aware that Confederate prisoners started arriving at the prison in February?" Both of these were said more in the manner of statement than question. Since Rob was aware of the camp and its intended purpose, he merely nodded in the affirmative.

Pinkerton continued, "We have an opportunity to get some really top-notch inside information about plans and certain activities taking place inside the Confederacy–perhaps even a few outside the Confederacy, but having a great bearing on the South's intentions. If we can secure good intelligence, it could affect the whole outcome of this war." He slapped his hand briskly on his desk for emphasis while continuing to gaze steadily at Rob. "How'd ya' like t' have a hand in ending this bloody war, lad, and without even totin' yer rifle?"

Rob considered the question, having a little trouble taking in what Pinkerton was proposing he do. "I'd like that fine, sir, though I don't see exactly what it is ya would have me do." His voice trailed off as he revealed his puzzlement and doubt.

He imagined that it was being suggested he go into the prison pretending to be a captured Confederate prisoner and could not see how that would work. He knew nothing of the rebel forces, their commanders nor troop movements. His Irish brogue would not give away his allegiance, since there were many immigrants on both sides of the issue. Even so, his suitability for such an assignment seemed questionable in his mind. He chose to keep his thoughts to himself to see what the boss would ask him to do.

"Have you ever heard of the Knights of the Golden Circle?" Pinkerton asked directly.

"Name's familiar, but I don't know hardly anything about 'em," came the reply. Rob had heard the name of the organization in conjunction with Copperheads–Southern sympathizers living in the North. "I've heard they're a secret group an' they oppose the North's invasion of the South, at least politically and philosophically. I'm guessin', they're secessionists."

Pinkerton was quick to take back the reins of the conversation. "Darned right they're secessionists. They've funded most of the Rebels' weapons, uniforms an' a good deal more besides. If we could round up some of the wealthy leaders, we might be able ta shut the whole organization down. But we'll need good information and evidence, lad, evidence. Either that or something that'll lead us ta the evidence we need." With that Pinkerton leaned back a little in his chair to let his words sink in. Then he went on again with, "I propose t' put you in the military prison as a civilian arrested for treasonous activities with the KGC. Once yer in an' the word of yer association with the Knights gets around, they'll be coming t' you."

Rob was thoughtful again for a short while. He commented, "Seems that could work." Then he asked, "How'll I know their talk or th' names o' those I should recognize?"

Pinkerton's smile broadened. "That's where their own secrecy will help you and us in our plan, Rob. We know the rituals and passwords–which you'll learn. But they won't expect ya t' talk about other members of your knowin'. That's against their own code. We'll have another agent inside with ya' at the same time. Just in case. Pretend not t' know each other apart from your KGC activities."

"An' who might that be, sir? Someone from th' agency, then?"

"John Ferguson, Molly's older brother, as ya trained with when ya first joined us. He's been in other parts of Illinois and Kentucky on assignments and was arrested last week at a Temple meeting he had infiltrated in Cairo. We arranged ta let him be taken ta the prison with the others and then got word to 'im of this plan. He's just layin' low until we get ya' in there with further instructions. Ya' should be able t' work together and watch each other's backs." The detective chief seemed pleased with himself.

"He's a good man in a scrape, I'll warrant. He knows how t' handle himself. What'll be my cover goin' in?"

"We figured it would be best for ya' ta pose as a newer member of one of the Temples in the St. Louis area. Y'll be brought in as a successful business owner from Granite City, whose family operates a headstone quarry. Yer sympathies are with the Southern cause. Ya've been giving lots of money ta see yer political wishes come ta pass an' help the Confederates equip themselves. Most of the prisoners came from the fightin' at Shiloh an' Corinth–mostly from Mississippi, Arkansas, Alabama an' Tennessee. There's no one in the prison yet from the St. Louis area an' we'll keep screening all new prisoners t' keep any others out while yer inside. This way there'll be none t' doubt your story. What d'ya' think of that, eh?" Pinkerton's grin showed his pleasure with his brain child.

"Sir, I think y've got yerself an agent an' I've got myself a job." Rob was already warming to this idea for his new assignment. He had no objection to gathering information covertly to help the Union's cause and knew Ferguson well enough to have a kernel of confidence in him as a working partner in this scheme. Also, his earlier comment about the man had been true. John Ferguson could handle himself in a fight–fair or otherwise. He'd be good to have around should things heat up during the mission.

Mr. Pinkerton further explained that Theobald Forrester, the St. Louis accountant, had provided enough contact information about the Knights of the Golden Circle that Pinkerton and a few of his agents were able to get good details of the organization's structure as well as a few names of influential members from that area. Armed with those facts, the agency had pursued a few of the more active Temples and lodges across southern Illinois and western and even central Kentucky. John Ferguson had been part of the team involved in those activities and had succeeded in infiltrating the Cairo group about six weeks earlier. His arrest along with the real members of that lodge had worked out to provide this opportunity perfectly.

If Finn and Ferguson could find out who the real kingpins of the Knights were, arrest warrants could be had and the Pinkertons would deal a crippling blow to a major funding source of the South. Rob knew this was the possibility, the goal of this mission. And he liked the fact that he would not be assassinating anyone in cold blood. This meeting was clearly at an end, so Rob stood and asked, "When an' where do I begin, Mr. Pinkerton?"

"Molly's got the details of yer cover an' a few other items y'll be needing," he answered. "She's done a good job of pulling a lot o' stuff together on this. She's got a lot at stake in it with her brother an' all."

And indeed she did. Three days later, an unshaven Rob Finn, using his own name but wearing a nice suit which had been deliberately made to look uncared for, gentleman's boots that were scuffed, and a crinkled crown derby hat, was escorted into the prison by uniformed provost guards. The elaborately faked pat-down at the gates failed to find either the knife or the cosh he carried secreted on his person. Due to his size, strength and the outcome of fights he had been in while on agency business in the past, he protested the need for the weapons. But Pinkerton had been adamant they be carried for protection, so Rob yielded the point.

It didn't take long to learn the wisdom of his mentor's insistence.

# CHAPTER FOUR

# Camp Douglas Prison

*Monday, July 14th, 1862*
*Within the enclosure of Camp Douglas Prison; Chicago's South*
*Side near Lake Michigan*

A portion of the 80 acres upon which what was to become the North's most notorious and inhumane prisoner of war camp had been donated by none other than the famous Senator Stephan Douglas, the "little giant" who had debated Abraham Lincoln during the 1858 debates. He had also prevailed over Lincoln in the 1859 Illinois senatorial election. Douglas died suddenly in 1861, lending his name to the site before the camp was turned to its prisoner-of-war role. Prior to that conversion, it was a facility for training new troops in the Union effort.

By the summer of 1862, the camp was being transitioned into its new role. Roughly half of the acreage was training grounds and half was enclosed for imprisonment, surrounded by a tall wire and post fence. The barracks buildings intended for prisoners, though newly completed, were shabby. Inadequate sewage handling, personal hygiene considerations and overall sanitation filled the air with an unpleasant stench. The Union guards tended to stay away from the perimeters of the fenced areas in order to avoid the fetid aromas.

The portion already converted held war prisoners captured from the battlefields as well as civilian sympathizers with the rebel cause. To most eyes, it was strange to see uniformed recruits practicing marching and battlefield commands immediately alongside enemy prisoners with only a fence separating the two. But for Rob and John, and their mission, it provided two things: an additional level of security overwatch and a ready, simple path of communication to those outside the camp.

None of which would have mattered, had the two spies not run into trouble almost as soon as Rob made his appearance there. Ferguson, upon his arrival and Rob upon his, had been discreetly pointed out to several officers of the guard detail. Careful instructions for the men's safety had been given, but for reasons of secrecy, not many members among the company of guards could be given those extra instructions nor the reasons they were necessary. From these conditions a misunderstanding arose which could have turned out much worse for Rob and John that what it did.

Though John was larger than the average man, he was nowhere near Rob's size. They agreed that it would be best for

John to continue handling messages through the fence, as he would be less conspicuous and memorable than Rob. Ferguson was in the process of handing over his daily note to Corporal Dixon, on the second day of their joint incarceration. Another guard, unaware of what was really taking place, reacted to seeing John's hand snake quickly through the fence and return. This second guard assumed the worst–that John was trying to stab or otherwise injure the bluebelly guard nearest the fence.

"You there! Step back or I'll shoot!" shouted the young guard, who then cocked the hammer back as he aimed his rifle at Ferguson. Judging by his fresh-faced looks and lanky frame, he was probably not more than eighteen or nineteen years old, much younger than the others on guard duty. Which made no difference to John when he turned and found himself in direct line with the soldier's aimed rifle. He quickly took a step back from the fence, raising his hands at the same time. He thought that the youngster might be more prone to brash or stupid action because of his youth and inexperience.

As John continued backing away, his challenger advanced toward him, finally stopping at the wire fence that separated them. With the rifle still pointed at Ferguson's chest, he continued in his demanding tone, "What do ya' think yer doing there, Reb? Trying to pick my corporal's pocket? What's that in yer hand? C'mon now, turn it over!" Ferguson swallowed hard, realizing that the folded paper he was palming in his right hand had been spotted.

The corporal had quickly stepped to the young soldier's side. With a quick move of his right arm he deflected the rifle upward, which caused it to fire. The bullet travelled safely, well above the men and the buildings, in the direction of nearby Lake Michigan. "At ease, Johnson! Return to your post! I've got things under control here."

The authority in the corporal's commands invited no discussion. The young private, looking puzzled and a little relieved, turned and carried the now emptied rifle at port arms. He strode across the compound, away from the incident which had drawn the attention of all within earshot.

Rob had been watching the events unfold from his vantage point across the yard within one of the few shaded areas available at that time of day. For several tense moments he had been fingering the cosh in his pocket, not sure what he would do to aid his partner should the need arise. As the young soldier stalked off from the scene of the confrontation, Rob was inwardly relieved.

His relief was short-lived, however. His eye caught two of the known KGCers hot-footing it over to Howell Gibbons, one of their leaders. Finn watched intently as their heads bobbed and arms pointed while they spoke with obvious excitement. He surmised that their discussion revolved around the just-completed incident involving Ferguson.

Trying to hide his concern, Rob shambled toward the small gathering, arriving in time to hear Gibbons remark, "Maybe we should soften 'im up a bit. Find out what he really knows. Let's get that paper from him first." Gibbons looked up and, seeing Rob, ceased his part in the conversation. Though he had been accepted as being a Knight by using their signs and code-words, Rob was a newcomer and, as such, not totally trusted by those who'd been together since before he arrived.

Rob tried to think of how he might help Ferguson avoid trouble. He said, "I think Ferguson trusts me. I'll get that note from him." Before he could add anything further, Gibbons said, "Not without a witness or two, you won't."

There would be no getting around the other man's assertion. Gibbons was the acknowledged leader of the KGC members within the prison and John Ferguson had just been seen passing or receiving a note from a guard; many pairs of eyes were witness to that fact. The enthusiastic intervention by the young Union private had seen to that.

Rob's mind was racing to find anything he could to keep Ferguson out of harm's way, but realized there was little he could do. He decided to let the episode play out a while longer. "Whatever you say, Gibbons. You're the boss." And with a non-committal shrug he set off to intercept Ferguson who was fast approaching an open end of the prisoner's barracks. Gibbons and his two followers were close on his heels.

"Hold up a second there, John," Rob called out with much more calm in his voice than he was feeling in his mind. "I'd like a word with ya."

Ferguson's face showed relief upon hearing Rob's voice. Then, looking past Rob at the others coming up, he showed forth puzzlement. He replied flatly, "What do you want with me?" With that, he stopped, planted his feet and braced himself for whatever physical attack might come. Rob was trying his best to communicate non-verbally with his friend and co-worker that he'd best play along. Together they'd find a way out of this jamb, or so he hoped.

"I'd like t' see that note yer carryin'," Rob answered. "Everybody saw ya had it in your hand when you came away from the fence."

"Then everybody can damn well see it now, too!"

Ferguson threw the folded-up square of paper at Rob's feet and veered to step around him, continuing on his way to the barracks. Gibbons' two companions quickly apprehended him, each taking one of Ferguson's shoulders and elbows in hand to control him. He did not resist their holds. It was likely he could have broken free had that been his wish. Instead, he stood in place, glaring at those around him and said, "If you had any brains, you would take this inside." His eyes were fixed on Gibbons as he delivered these words.

Rob had scooped up the note, which he was holding carefully so as not to arouse any further suspicion, and, upon hearing Ferguson's suggestion, agreed. He switched the note to his left hand and retrieved the cosh from his pocket with his right. Making no attempt to conceal the small leather weapon in his massive hand from his onlookers, his real meaning was quite clear as he said, "Yeah. Let's get out of the sun." He turned and entered the building with the small train of followers close behind. The note was still folded, there had been no way for him to open it privately to learn of its contents before the rest of the men formed around him. Sensing that Ferguson posed no threat, his captors had released him before they entered the building, though they stayed within arm's reach, should he decide to try to escape.

Howell Gibbons, shorter and older than either Ferguson or Finn, wore a full beard traced with a few gray strands, as was the chestnut brown hair at his temples. He held out his hand to Rob, indicating that the latter should surrender the note, which he did. As Gibbons carefully unfolded the document, Rob was preparing himself mentally for whatever might come next. The cosh remained in his hand for all to see; the knife hidden in his boot would come out the instant it was needed. He noticed that Ferguson seemed quite calm and was puzzled by that behavior.

Was John really that unflappable? Was he ready for what had to come next?

Turning the unfolded note in his hands several times, Gibbons announced, "It's blank; empty. Doesn't say a damned thing!" His surprise, bordering on disappointment, was plain for all to see. "This some kind of game is it, Ferguson?" he now demanded to know.

"Same game as always, Gibbons. Just because you didn't know about it doesn't make it any less real. Jerry Dixon's one of us, helped start the Lodge over in Effingham, if you must know. I was ordered by Mr. Hunt himself to communicate at least weekly through the man. Finn and I are here to make sure the Yanks don't put any spies in with us. When I've got nothin' to report, I give 'em a blank. When there's no change in orders, they give me a blank. An' that's the way it's been the while I've been here." His delivery of this explanation was as cool as if he'd been reading a recipe to a kitchen maid. No emotion involved; an impressive feat for the sometimes fiery Scot.

The hush of the small gathering lasted for some time. What had just been revealed to them was unexpected and probably shocking to Gibbons and the others. While not totally surprised by Ferguson's words, Rob was certainly impressed by them. John had remained calm while he fabricated the addition to their cover stories that would assure their safety for at least a while longer. And it had been delivered with the convincing calmness of a professional actor on the stage. Further, it seemed obvious the Knights, or 'brothers,' hearing it, including Gibbons, were taken in, perhaps even somewhat in awe upon learning of John's claimed connection between himself, Rob, and the well-known Charles Hunt. Hunt was among the highest echelons of KGC leaders, as well as one of their chief financial backers from St. Louis. In Rob's estimation, the entire ruse was a stroke of genius. He couldn't wait until the next time he and John were alone to thank and congratulate the man.

What would happen next would be predictable, thought Rob. Word would spread among the prisoners in the camp, raising everyone's esteem of the two Pinkerton spies in their midst as they regarded them highly–the direct result of falling for John's story under duress. Their newly feigned positions and connections within the subversive and secret pro-Confederacy organization would likely be their ticket into the KGC inner circle at Camp Douglas. This might be just the break that the two men where hoping to develop. In any event, they would need to be doubly cautious now. They didn't need their new story being told beyond the confines of the prison, lest it fall on ears that knew and could prove it to be false.

The windfall of information that followed was not long in developing. Within three days of this incident, John and Rob had collected the names of not only all the KGC members and sympathizers within the camp, but also of many of its leaders and organizers in the civilian populations in Illinois, Indiana, Kentucky and Missouri. Since it was now expected by those watching from the prisoner's side of the fence, Ferguson's foray to carry his messages to Corporal Dixon were regarded lightly. Little did they suspect the content of those notes was precisely what they would most have feared. It revealed who the subversives were and what they were up to. So rather than helping the KGC in its plan to thwart the Union cause, the notes were instead helping the Union build its case against key Confederate sympathizers in the North.

Rob had indeed communicated his praise of Ferguson's quick-thinking, first to John himself and then in a tiny note to Pinkerton, which Ferguson himself had unwittingly passed through the fence along with the other communiqués that Dixon carried. John would have omitted the details of his deft fabrication. As he had told Rob, he'd had plenty of time to concoct the notion of the corporal's KGC connection earlier, when he had first arrived in the camp. He knew a ready-made explanation would come in handy, should he ever be spotted by the other prisoners. As things happened, it worked out better than he had hoped and better than he could have planned.

The information that they passed back to Pinkerton was sufficient to arrest and incarcerate dozens of those implicated by the spy team's messages. Pinkerton knew he needed to get his boys out of their present assignment before the next phase of the operation took place.

# The Joy Of Deliverance

*Saturday, July 19th, 1862*
*The Pinkerton Agency Offices, Downtown Chicago*

Working himself and his staff late into the evening in order to complete all the telegrams and written documents that would be needed, Allan Pinkerton left the office for home. He was completely satisfied that they had taken all necessary steps for withdrawing his two agents from the prison. They would be safely and quietly taken from the prison in the morning and returned to the Agency's offices for further debriefing. Rob would have been inside only one week. As they were leaving the agency's offices together, Molly Ferguson turned to Pinkerton with smiling face and flashing eyes and said, "I am so happy that John will be getting out tomorrow, Mr. Pinkerton. It just scared me to think where he was and the kind of criminals he was living with. I'll be so glad to be seeing him again tomorrow!"

That was the plan, anyway.

*Sunday, July 20th, 1862*
*Camp Douglas Prison, Chicago, Illinois*

Through their earlier arrangement, it was understood between the Commandant of Camp Douglas, the Provost Marshall of the Union Army for the District of Chicago, Corporal Jeremiah Dixon and Allan Pinkerton that Corporal Dixon would handle all official and less-than-official dealings with the two agent-prisoners while they were at Camp Douglas. Thus all of them expected the corporal to receive the release orders and act upon them without question. No one could have anticipated that the man's appendix would inflame and enlarge that night, rendering him unfit for duty in the morning as he was prepared for surgery. Dixon had no idea this would be the day of the spies' intended release and could not intervene to select his own replacement.

As fate would have it, there was no other non-commissioned officer available to fill in for Corporal Dixon. Without giving it too much thought, that morning's Officer-of-the-Guard glanced at the message informing him of Dixon's unsuitability to report for duty, quickly perused the yard guards duty roster for the day and selected Private Alvin Johnson to stand in for the ailing corporal. His only reason for the selection being that the private's surname and his were the same: Johnson.

As far as he knew, they were not related. But he liked coinci-
dences–considered them "good omens," and made his selection
accordingly. No one would question the aging lieutenant's
judgement. No one would care. Besides which, it would do the
youngster a world of good to have the additional responsibilities
of the corporal's position temporarily on his shoulders. It would
show what kind of stuff the kid was made of.

Lieutenant Johnson waddled unceremoniously out of the
watch office without really paying any attention to the orders-of-
the-day that he was carrying. He didn't see them as being his particular responsibility; they were matters for the enlisted men to
worry about. He hadn't bothered to read them. Their details
bored him. His place was to assign jobs and sort out conflicts
when they arose, not wipe the noses of a bunch of overexcited
men in uniforms. He had grabbed the armband with two chevrons of pale blue, signifying a temporary rank when worn on the
sleeve of the soldier's tunic. He also took the gunbelt with its
holstered revolver down from the wall peg on which it was hung.
It was the other sign of office of corporal of the guard. "This
ought'a make the little bastard happy," the lieutenant thought to
himself, though he had no particular reason to want to reward
the private with happiness. Just an idle thought flitting through.
Oh Sundays....

Seeing the morning detail already loosely formed up in
ranks on the portion of the parade ground designated for roll call,

as he navigated to the front of the formation, Lieutenant Johnson inhaled and bellowed in his best command voice, "Private Johnson! Front and center!"

Upon hearing his name called, the young soldier had come to attention. As soon as the command was uttered he marched as smartly as he knew how to complete it. He was uncertain what the officer could want. The private's recent embarrassment involving the discharged rifle and chastisement by his corporal was still a sore spot for him and he worried this could somehow be connected. Nothing could have surprised him more than when Lieutenant Johnson announced, "Johnson, you will take over temporarily as corporal of the guard." Handing the armband, the gunbelt and the written orders to the stunned lad, he completed the assignment by saying, "You are acting corporal, you have the duty, take charge of your troops!" And with that the chubby officer grabbed Johnson's rifle and exited the field without decorum and without concern. As far as he was concerned, he had done his duty and could find someplace quiet to spend the rest of his day.

Meanwhile, Private Johnson was feeling pretty good about himself. Carefully positioning the gunbelt around his sparse hips, he then slid the armband of office up his sleeve to a point midway between elbow and shoulder. Certain that he looked the part, he called the small group of rifle-carrying guards to attention. He then proceeded to call out what commands he could think of to march them to their duty stations, not noticing too much that his errant directions were the cause of more than one misstep by the uniformed guards. The men themselves weren't overly concerned with his performance nor their own. No one else seemed to notice the poorly executed drill. Acting Corporal Johnson decided that he'd done well and, pleased with that thought, sat in the shade on Dixon's usual spot, a folding stool. He opened the sheaf of papers and ran his eyes over them, his lips moving as he slowly read their contents.

When he came to the third order for that day, "Concerning Prisoners to be Released," he read the instructions carefully, not having been part of such a procedure previously. He did not recognize the names of the four men being released that day, which came as no surprise. He knew almost none of the prisoners by name. Not only was he the newest guard within the company, he avoided the prisoners and getting to know them. He thought of them as disgusting and beneath deserving his attention. He didn't mind his job as a prison guard as long as he didn't have to get close enough to smell the vile, dirty men or listen to their constant cursing and complaining.

Johnson was ready when the release detail arrived from outside the camp. These were men who had been in uniform for some time. Their sergeant was immaculate in his uniform and rigid in his bearing. There were no mistakes in his commands;

no missteps by his four subordinates, who were also immaculate in their uniforms.

Johnson fell in step behind the group as it approached the transfer gate in the fence. He wanted to see how professional soldiers conducted themselves while on duty. He wished to mimic them in order to seem more professional.

He was impressed with the way their movements were all in unison, with how they executed the sergeant's commands crisply and perfectly. He heard the sergeant's voice ringing clearly as he read off his orders and named the four men being released to his charge. That man had a wonderful command voice. Johnson was sure his own voice would be much like the sergeant's with just a little more practice. Perhaps even by the time Dixon came back on duty, if only the man would stay gone for a few days. Who knew? Anything could happen.

Rob Finn and John Ferguson had been informed that morning before breakfast that their release papers had been secured, and told to be ready to leave the camp when the provost marshall's release detail arrived. After breakfast, the two went quickly to work gathering their few personal items. They used extra care making certain they'd left behind no traces of their real mission. Both were satisfied that none of the other prisoners could find anything to implicate them. That did not mean there would be no suspicion or speculation attached to their sudden and early release. Both men were aware they could not afford to unexpectedly run into their former "fellow prisoners" again without complications. But what were the chances of that happening?

Rob and John spotted the provost's release detail just inside the fence as soon as they exited the barracks building they had been clearing out of. They also saw two other prisoners like themselves hastening in the direction of the detail. Delighted at the prospect of their imminent release, the grins on their faces spread wide as they hurried to join the small formation that would take them outside the gates to freedom.

Private Johnson took his eyes off the provost's detail in time to see two prisoners emerge from the near end of the closest prisoner barracks. Wasn't the shorter one the same man who had been the source of his own embarrassment just several days earlier? How it could be that a trouble maker like that was being released? Mindful of his new position, and calling upon what little military training he'd actually had, he handled the papers as best he could. He was certain that he looked very military and proper to anyone watching.

The provost's detail, at their sergeant's precise command, formed around the prisoners, executed a perfect "About Face" command and proceeded to march out through the gate they had so recently entered. When they stopped in front of Acting Corporal Johnson, he was still struggling to re-read the portion of the orders which were his obligation. He actually twitched when the seasoned sergeant before him barked, "Release detail reporting for prisoner identification as ordered." The sergeant did not append the word "sir" to his report, as there was no way he could humble himself to thus refer to the pimply-faced teenager in front of him.

Johnson nodded in the affirmative and managed to squeak out, "Please carry on, sergeant," hoping against all odds that he had the words right. He continued to scan the sheet in his hand to find what his next responsibility might be, when from behind him he heard a booming voice declare, "John Ferguson! Whatever are you doing here ... and ... dressed like that?!" From his peripheral vision, the acting corporal saw a man in minister's garb approaching from behind and to his right. The signs of recognition and surprise on the man's face and in his voice were so obviously genuine that he never paused to consider otherwise. Meanwhile, Ferguson was making all manner of hand and facial gesticulations in a failed attempt to cut short the minister's unwanted greeting. Doing so had the effect of drawing all eyes to himself, intentional or not.

Alvin Johnson had never found it easy to get along with others. A misfit in school and unpopular with the girls, he had enlisted as soon as the Army recruiter would have him. He lied about his age in order to be accepted. Alvin was able to read, though not as well as some others he'd been to school with. In training camp, the old routines of being made fun of and name-calling had returned. There was not a single man of his training class that Johnson could consider a true friend.

The non-coms in charge of his class were only too glad to get rid of Alvin when the prison camp had asked if they had anyone ready for 'early graduation.'

Thus it was that a poorly-trained, under-aged, friendless, poorly-educated and unintelligent youngster found himself in a position of authority for which he had no experience and little grasp. Determined to succeed in this present duty he resolved to show all present that he was capable of being in charge.

Acting Corporal Johnson knew full well that, should a prisoner escape while he was in charge of the guard detail, he would be branded a failure and again be a laughing stock for others. His normally dull senses went on high alert at the minister's outburst and Ferguson's actions. Johnson was neither bright enough nor experienced enough to realize that no danger of escape existed. After all, this was a prisoner release. Alvin knew he was supposed to verify the identity of every prisoner being released. That was the very thing he was preparing to do when the minister had recognized one of the prisoners as not belonging. Alvin began to panic. Something was wrong! He had to do something before the man got outside the camp!

Sergeant Heath's detail remained halted in formation and at attention. Passing around the sergeant and his men, Johnson moved quickly to where Ferguson now stood. Johnson had managed to fumble the revolver from its holster by the time he reached the prisoner. He cocked the hammer as he raised the gun and aimed it at Ferguson's chest. His panic was multiplied by his recent embarrassment involving this same prisoner, and the fact that he wasn't sure what was taking place, and that he did not wish to be made fool of for the second time in a week.

Young Alvin Johnson was always afraid of being out-smarted. He felt he was on the verge of losing control of this situation, of messing up. Certain that if he acted quickly enough, he could avoid both, he shouted, "Halt right there! Not another word or step until this is sorted out!"

Angered by the stupidity of the young soldier holding him at gun point, and anxious to remove the provost's detail and the other prisoners from the line of fire, Ferguson made an impetu-ously stupid move. He lurched to the outside of the detail, past the provost man on his left, expecting to be able to clear every-thing up with a few words of explanation between himself, the acting corporal and the Reverend Frasier.

The barrel of the pistol was eighteen inches from John Ferguson's head when a surprised Acting Corporal Johnson jerked the trigger. The bullet made a perfectly round hole in John's forehead and took a large portion of the back of his head completely off. He was dead where he fell.

The resulting chaos was complete. The black-clad man of God, whose surprised exclamation had unwittingly initiated the fatal chain of events, rushed toward the deceased, muttering, "Oh God, no!" repeatedly, his shock overwhelming his ministerial calm. Sergeant Heath positioned his men to contain the remaining prisoners and hold off the small but growing crowd of onlookers. Heath then took further command and ordered several of the Union soldiers employed as guards to arrest Acting Corporal Johnson and hold him pending further investigation. Heath was certain that not much investigation would be needed, other than to figure what idiot had placed the youngster in charge of the guard detail.

Meanwhile, Rob sank to his knees alongside his friend, reaching over to grasp his hand one last time. Grief had been his constant companion for many weeks after his sons and wife had died, and threatened now to return. He recognized the emotional grip of sorrow, and pushed it away. He would never again allow himself to be swallowed up in that maelstrom. He was stronger now and wiser.

It was not that he did not care, nor was he unfeeling. Rather than dwell on what he could not change, tragic though it was, he knew that the better course was to press on with whatever jobs and needs were still before him. Though shocked and saddened by Ferguson's unexpected death, he also resolved again in that moment not to be overwhelmed by emotions. Having to face Molly back at the office would be difficult enough. That young woman was genuinely attached to her brother. She would be crushed by his sudden passing. It was an unimaginable chain of events that had led up to it.

The prison's commandant, together with Lieutenant Johnson and Sergeant Heath, had taken the revolver from Acting Corporal Johnson and marched him inside the watch office. The men of the provost's detail stood guard over the remaining three prisoners including Rob. It was not many minutes before Sergeant Heath returned and told the prisoners they were free to go. Rob watched the other two vacate the premises. There were other flurries of activity involving prison staff members hurrying between buildings while looking at nothing and no one in particular.

Rob was not surprised when he saw Allan Pinkerton's coach pull up a short time later. There was a telegraph key in the office of the prison; the Pinkerton offices, which were not terribly far from the prison, had just had a listening key installed for their own use. Though they could not send from their office, they could receive all traffic, and even had their own 'address' code for messages being wired to them. What Rob was not prepared for was seeing Molly also step down from the coach behind their employer. She had been the person to receive and transcribe the telegraphed message from the prison which said, "Come at once. Accident, your man Ferguson hurt." The key operator who had sent the message was unaware of the real extent of the bullet's damage.

CHAPTER SIX

# Saint Louis Knights

*Early Tuesday evening, August 5th, 1862*
*Planters Hotel Lobby, St. Louis, Missouri*

Rob had received further training in the secret words and signs used by the Knights of the Golden Circle. His cover now, using his real name, was as the protégé of a wealthy Chicago financier wishing to support the movement while remaining anonymous. Pinkerton had provided him with St. Louis area locations and names of people he was to meet. For this assignment he would work alone.

He was not yet fully comfortable in the newly-tailored suits provided by rush order through Pinkerton's connections. The clothing fit well enough; it was rather a matter of Rob's being unaccustomed to the cut and finery of what he was wearing. Everything he had on, right down to the new boots, had been cut and sewn to his personal measurements by professionals. His Colt Pocket Pistol and boot knife were so well hidden that it was as though his outfit had been made for them, too. Which, of course, it had.

Rob knew nothing about art, other than what caught his eye, and he was regarding a beautiful oil painting of a landscape which hung across from where he perched on one of the lobby sofas. The hotel lobby provided ample space for guests and visitors. It was a huge room, lushly appointed. His eyes were constantly scanning the room's activity. Rob spotted his contact from the moment the man entered the building. Their flitting eye-contact and the slight sign and counter-sign finger movements confirmed the positive identification of each other to both men. Rob stood to greet the broad-shouldered, blonde, bearded man who approached him with right hand out-stretched. He was only slightly shorter than Rob; this description, together with the signs already passed, removed any doubt of positive identification.

"Rob Finn, it has been too long since last we met," exclaimed Jeffrey Heinz as they grasped each other's hands and shook a gentlemanly greeting. Heinz's smile was ear-to-ear, selling the authenticity of this meeting between two old friends to any who might be watching.

"How've ya been, yersel', Jeff?" Rob asked easily, as though he really had been missing an old acquaintance. "Ya look no worse for wear!" he added, also smiling widely.

"I'm very, very good Rob, and even better now you're here." His welcome and relief at their meeting seemed entirely genuine to Rob as well as any on-lookers. And why shouldn't he be happy to see the man who was supposed to be bringing him drafts for many thousands of dollars from Yankee banks to help swell the coffers of the Confederacy? "Shall we dine first, or perhaps even conduct our business during dinner?" The question came forth as naturally as the rest of the charade had gone thus far.

Rob considered the hotel dining room to be about as safe a place for their conversation as any he might otherwise imagine. It was public and yet had booths tucked into corners affording privacy. He'd been in the city and the hotel for two nights already and knew the layout of things well. There were two other Pinkerton agents present in the same hotel even now, he knew. This scheme was part of Pinkerton's elaborate plans for keeping his agents safe while on assignment. He could not recognize the two men watching over him; he had no description, drawing or picture of either, and he'd never met them.

With this in mind, Rob quickly agreed they should conduct business while they ate by saying, "I always try t' mix a bit o' business with pleasure. I'll get us a table with some privacy. Please, come along." And he headed into the open french doors leading into the dining room. He was recognized at once by the maître d'hôtel who was happy to oblige their need.

During dinner, the two men discussed the needs for equipment and supplies, never actually mentioning guns, ammunition, uniforms, tents or similar provisions for an army in the field. Heinz described that there were growing needs in the central portion of Kentucky, though never mentioned exactly where and did not offer any details of troop movements or numbers. He did let slip that a General Smith would be counting on being well-supplied enough to handle the Union forces. This was all spoken in low voice and a good distance away from any staff or patrons of the restaurant.

Following his orders as perfectly as he was able, Rob passed the bank drafts to his dinner companion. There were two of them, each in the amount of $50,000 drawn on the First National Bank of St. Louis County. Heinz's face beamed anew as he read the amounts on each of the drafts. "This'll go a long way to advance the cause, Rob! A long way! You have no idea how much this will help, especially just now." Jeff's obvious enthusiasm and sincerity toward the cause he believed in were genuine.

Jeff Heinz was probably a few years Rob's junior, and was also a farmer in the area. His family owned large agricultural holdings that they worked using a combination of family members, hired hands, and tenant share-croppers. It came out in conversation that Jeff and his father were completely opposed to slavery of any sort. Jeff stated that he firmly opposed all oppressors.

The comment took Rob by surprise, which he showed by asking, "If ya dislike slavery, then why support the Confederacy?" He did so without any judgement or emotion.

Heinz's answer surprised him even more. "It's never been about the slavery, Rob. It's about States' rights for self-rule and the right to secede at any time. Those were supposed to be guaranteed by the Constitution. Lincoln's election and claiming ownership of all 'Federal' sites within the states prove that he and those that go along with him are no better than tyrants and dictators. Slavery! Slavery will be done away with of its own accord in this generation. It can't continue and even the slave owners know that much. No sir. This war isn't about slavery, much as the politicians of the North want us to believe that. It's more about a government usurping powers and authority the people never intended it to have."

Jeff Heinz delivered this message with passion but no anger.

Clinging to his pretended position of support for the Confederacy, Rob found himself thinking for the first time in his life that he might actually agree with the thoughts just been laid before him. He himself had been drawn into the Abolitionist Movement before the war started. The emotional rhetoric used by leaders of that movement had preyed upon his heart and mind. He felt strongly that no human being had the right to own or control another. Now he was being told that many Southerners, even some slave owners, felt the same way. How could this be, he wondered? Naturally, he shared none of what he was thinking with Jeff. Outwardly he continued to pretend to support slavery and the Confederacy.

Bringing himself back into the moment with an effort, Rob resumed by saying, "Yer right of course. The Federals have no business telling the states what we can an' can't do. Death t' tyrants!" Though he emphasized this last phrase, he was careful to keep his voice down for fear of being overheard. And yet, there was something almost freeing when he heard this motto of the KGC being spoken in his own voice.

"Death to tyrants," agreed Jeff, repeating the KGC rallying cry as he stood up from the table. "And the end of this war cannot come quickly enough!" This man did not behave as someone who wanted a protracted war just to destroy other people or their property, nor to prove any personal point of view he might hold.

Rob could not help but like the man. He felt he had made a friend and then thinking that his feeling was foolish. He himself was employed and working to destroy the KGC and the secessionist Rebel movement with it. He had already killed several men while working under orders to do just that.

To say he was in the throes of self-conflict at this moment would have been an understatement.

Meeting and speaking with other ranking members of the KGC in St. Louis was another piece of his present mission there, so he reminded Jeff that, in order to continue the influx of money coming from his patron, he would need to meet others and learn of their plans to overturn the Union's current aggression toward the South. Rob hoped the inner turmoil he felt was not obvious to the other man.

"We'll need to be careful, Rob, though we can get it done," Jeff continued in hushed tones. "No one wants to be found out, which I'm sure you understand. So it'll take me another two or three days to get things arranged. Will you still be here that long?"

"Yes, o' course. My patron wouldn't want me t' go back t' Chicago before getting as much information about the local operations as possible," Rob replied. Regarding Pinkerton as his patron, at least he had finally told the truth. "He can't be expected t' continue t' fund a thing unless he believes the men involved an' their goals are worth the investment." Again he was speaking the truth though it was veiled in deception.

"Nor would we expect him to, Rob. It'll take me that long to make my report personally to those involved. I'll deposit those drafts into two different banks under different names so I'll have the deposit slips to show. Then I'll tell them individually about our conversation and my thoughts about you, which are all good, by the way."

Rob felt a twinge of guilt at drawing this good man in, gathering information that might be used to arrest, confine and eventually try him and his friends in the Federal Court system. "An' I will have a similar report for my employer," Rob rejoined, "

Includin' similar observations about yersel', Jeff. Ya can send a message confirmin' our next meetin' time an' place t' me here at the hotel. I won't be sendin' any wires back t' Chicago; too risky over the open telegraph." This last statement was an out-and-out lie. He would encode his message to Pinkerton in the way he'd been trained and have it into the agency the next morning. He thought it best they end their meeting without further socializing that evening. He needed time to process his feelings and thoughts.

"I guess I'll be seein' ya in a couple o' days then, Jeff. I'll be waitin' t' hear from ya–don't stretch me out, eh?" He smiled and offered his right hand. As they shook hands in parting, Rob added, "Til then, my friend." It was said sincerely, but Rob's stomach churned knowing the betrayal he had in mind.

Jeff's simple reply of, "Yes. Until then, friend," seemed equally sincere. The two men parted, looking forward to their next get- together. Heinz headed for the main doors out of the hotel. Rob headed for the staircase leading to his second floor room.

Rob found himself with a lot to think about when he reached his room and was alone to do so.

First, he had so many things to try to resolve at his home in Darien. He was sure that Cath and Maggie could manage the younger children, keeping them fed and clothed and clean and warm. He was not sure they could manage keeping from each other's throats. He was aware that Maggie had some kind of crush on him, one that would pass as soon as the right young suitor came along. She was young enough and pretty enough that there should be plenty such fellows along in the next couple of years. Cath was head-strong and would struggle more each passing day and week having to take orders from Maggie. Yet he'd had to make it clear when he left, that Maggie would be in charge of the household during his absences. He had been hoping to check in on the family before heading to St. Louis, after the prison assignment ended.

Then with Ferguson's unfortunate end had come a whole set of unexpected feelings and demands on his time. In the slightly over two weeks since John's death, Rob had not only had to get involved in more aspects of training newly-hired men, but also had many things to memorize for his own upcoming assignment. He further found himself spending a lot of time with Molly. For the first several days, Rob had been consoling her in her grief over John. Later on that week, their relationship had grown to being something else, he wasn't quite sure what. They were closer friends, for sure, and there was was mutual attraction between them. She was also younger than he, though not by as many years as Maggie. He had been thinking of Molly as a possible surrogate mother for his children, which was fair to none of them. They'd never even met. And yet, there was that attraction.

Added to all that was John's untimely death itself. Rob was pretty certain that invisible forces were regularly at work in human's lives; this was his notion of fate. Bridget had never approved of his position on this, and neither would any priest of the Roman Catholic Church. It didn't matter, though. What the Church taught about what happened over 1,800 years earlier seemed pretty far-fetched to him. He would have liked to believe it all as truth, he just could not find it in himself to do so. There were just too many times he had witnessed so-called good Christians behaving in ways that were opposite to their stated beliefs. It wasn't uncommon for priests to be just as guilty, in his experience.

He understood the Church's teachings about sin and forgiveness, but found them hard to accept. To Rob it seemed that a man made his own way, choosing right or wrong and reaping what consequences came from those choices. That seemed fair and right to him. As for fate? Who knew? He believed John Ferguson to have been a good person who lived a good life and tried to do right. Now John was dead before even reaching the age of thirty-five, no widow or children left behind. He had died quickly with little or no pain or fear and no dependents who would suffer due to his passing. That seemed pretty good to him. Bridget had led a very good life and ended badly, dying in unimaginable pain and grief. Their two boys had also suffered painful deaths.

How was a man to find God, and God's plan in all that? The priest had told him that God's ways are unfathomable to humans, words he had heard before. He didn't believe them before and he didn't believe them now. As far as Rob Finn was concerned, all the words of all the priests and bishops and other religious were merely ways of keeping the crowds under control. Those shepherds were the ones that Jesus had warned about in the Bible. They were the "blind guides" and the "clouds without rain", unable to deliver on the promises they regularly made to keep people coming to their weekly Masses.

Now he found himself on another dangerous assignment to gather incriminating evidence against powerful, wealthy and motivated people that he'd been told were the most fearsome enemies of the government he served. He'd been out of the stinking Camp Douglas Prison for less than three weeks. Three weeks during which he'd found himself helping to train new spies, and having feelings for his fallen friend's sister, worrying about his children and their care-provider, and also finding that he liked the first person he'd met in St. Louis as a contact among the KGC. Add to that his growing doubts regarding the right-ness of his allegiance to a system of political and financial control and his head was fairly spinning.

With such thoughts as these still rolling around in his head he finally drifted off to sleep. During the night his con-science poked its way into his dreams in which he imagined himself having a conversation with Saint Peter at the pearly gates of heaven. The trouble in his dream centered on Rob's having killed people who were doing nothing to him, save occupying the uniform of the enemy and being the target he'd been assigned to kill by his orders.

* * * *

*5:47 a.m., Wednesday, August 6th, 1862*
*Planters Hotel, St. Louis, Missouri*

When the sun's strong rays crept into his room's window between the slightly-parted drapes, he awoke refreshed and ready to face a new day. Rob was no longer content to mire himself in the sorrows of yesterday while there were yet things to be accomplished today. He was no longer the self-pitying hulk he had been a few months earlier.

After finishing his morning toilet and dressing, he went down to the dining room for breakfast, collecting a newspaper along the way. He enjoyed his perfectly cooked eggs and bacon and was lingering over his second cup of coffee when his eye found a small notice in the paper reading:

## Sons of Liberty
### *Unite against the Oppressors*

Meeting TONIGHT - Helms Grove - Starts at Dusk
All freedom-loving men Welcome!

This was exactly the kind of thing Rob thought he should attend to find as much about the pro-Confederacy and anti-Union activity in the area as he could. He didn't really know what to expect, but was well-versed in the secret words and signs of recognition that many of these secret groups were using. Often the words and signs were similar, if not actually identical. He figured that attending this would be a good use of his evening. On his way out of the dining room he asked the maitré d' for directions to Helms Grove. The man was able to oblige with simple directions to a large wooded area not too far from the downtown area.

His plan for the evening provided Rob a greater sense of purpose for the rest of this day and his mission. Upon returning to his room and securing the door, he took out his pistol and unloaded it, cleaned it and reloaded it. He wanted to be certain it was reliable should it be needed. He also drew his boot knife from its sheath and dressed the blade to razor sharpness. A man shouldn't take unnecessary chances when it came to his personal defense equipment. He wasn't taking any chances. His family was depending upon him to return home safely.

Almost as an afterthought he left the hotel and headed to another contact he'd been informed of as being reliable, Theo

Forrester. He knew he needed to be careful in his approach so as not to expose either of them to anyone watching their actions. He needed to show himself as an earnest young businessman looking for financial advice in the St. Louis area. The office he was looking for was easy enough to find. The outer door was unlocked, so he let himself into the outer room of the suite. There were two other clients seated, waiting their turn to see the accountant.

The clerk who came to the window was a young man much smaller than Rob. He was slender and had a worried, harried look about him. "How may we help you, sir?" the man asked without really looking at Rob. "I'm afraid Mr. Forrester is with someone just now and there are two others ahead of you." Rob had to decide which of his two calling cards he would use. From Pinkerton's briefing on the mission he was certain that Forrester was trustworthy. He knew nothing of the clerk before him. He couldn't use his Pinkerton Agency card without possibly giving away his real purpose in the city. He opted to remove a plain gentleman's card of white stock with his name, Robert Finn, being the only engraving on it.

"I only need a moment of his time. I believe our mutual friend told him to expect me?" Rob suggested this in the hope that the clerk would at least announce him. Perhaps Mr. Forrester would take the hint and accommodate him. It was worth the try. Any advice or warnings he could receive from Forrester

before attending a meeting with this KGC group would be helpful.

He held his derby hat carefully in his lap as he sat waiting
with the others. The door to the inner office opened and a
stately, elderly gentleman emerged walking with the aid of a
finely crafted cane. His waistcoat, vest and trousers were exqui-
site as was the silk top hat he placed smartly upon his head. The
person who followed him from the inner office announced, "I
should be able to have those accounts up-to-date and summarized
for you by the end of the week, Mr. Hunt. Let's say by noon on
Saturday, if that meets with your approval?" The white-haired
accountant smiled at his client in anticipation of an approving
reply.

"Saturday! Saturday's no good. I have to have them in
hand no later than Friday at noon!" His countenance had red-
dened a little and he was obviously displeased. "I was told you
were reliable, Forrester. Don't disappoint me." Hunt's final remark was still firm and demanding, though his passion was less.

"We'll do everything we can, Mr. Hunt. I'll see to it personally. Until Friday noon, then, sir. I bid you good day." He
turned to re-enter his private office. The clerk was close on his
heel carrying the calling card Rob had given him. They were se-
questered behind the closed door for only a moment when the
man named Forrester came back into the outer office and strode
to where he could face his waiting customers. "Mr. Deane and

Mr. Stiles, thank you for your patience. I will get to you in just a matter of moments. Would you be so kind to allow me just three minutes with this gentleman? He has traveled from Chicago to see me on an urgent matter. I promise not to keep you waiting beyond that. Will that be alright with you both?" The other two seated gentlemen looked at each other and Rob before turning back toward the accountant with their acquiescent shrugs and nods.

"Thank you so much for your understanding," Forrester effused. "We'll be done in just a few moments." With that he opened the pass gate through the counter and gestured for Rob to follow him. Within a few quick strides they were both seated in the private office with the door closed and facing one another.

The older man spoke first, "We'll dispense with pleasantries and all that usual claptrap. I know who you are and who you work for and have a good idea what your purpose in St. Louis may be. How can I help you?"

Rob had been pondering what kind of information would be most valuable to him for tonight's meeting, so he was prepared with his question, "Is there anyone or anything I need ta know about before I go t' a meeting at Helms Grove this evening, sir?"

"Helms Grove!?" Came the response charged with warning and dismay. Though said with urgency it was also the man's practiced quiet while conducting clandestine meetings in his business office that kept his voice from rising to a volume that would travel beyond the door. "What makes you think that'll be a good idea?"

Pinkerton had assured Rob that Theo Forrester was, in addition to being knowledgeable and trustworthy, a no-nonsense man. This first exchange between them confirmed that. Rob immediately liked the older man. He explained briefly about seeing the newspaper announcement of the meeting, and shared his need to gather names and other information pertaining to the local chapter of the KGC organization.

"Is there any particular reason that I shouldn't go?" Rob asked.

"None, so long as you have no plan to keep on livin'. There's a rough crowd among the lot that meets out there. No tellin' what they might do, were they to find out your true purpose. What's so important for you to find there?"

"We need t' know who is doin' the plannin', an' what their plans are. That'll allow us t' get ahead of 'em an' round 'em up before they can cause more mischief."

"Well, good luck to you, lad. The man you saw leaving as you came in is Mr. Charles Hunt. He's highly placed in the KGC. Don't know if he'll be there or not. He won't lay hands on you, but I'll wager there's several among his employees and followers who would. It wouldn't do for you to get found out. Trouble for everyone, even myself. I hope he didn't get a good look at you?"

"I don't think he even noticed me, sir. I was sittin' down when he walked past me an' he didn't appear t' pay me any attention."

"Good. If you're to go out there, it'd probably be best to go as a complete stranger to all. You must have a story you'd use about yourself?"

"Aye. Indeed I do, sir." Rob gave the briefest of details about his cover and his activities since arriving in St. Louis, including the previous evening's dinner with Jeff Heinz.

"Jeff's a good enough lad, though I can't imagine him throwin' in with that bunch. Keep an eye on him and the rest you come across. If you're determined to go out there, then I've no more to offer," Forrester said. "Keep your wits about you and may God bless your efforts."

"Thank ya for yer time, sir," said Rob as he made ready to leave the busy office. He had already used up the three minutes Mr. Forrester had promised his clients. They shook hands.

Forrester looked up to Rob's face and said, "Take good care of yourself, young man."

With that, Rob was headed out to the street where he donned his hat and strode quickly back to the hotel. He ate his early lunch alone.

Once back in his room, he reflected upon events of the past twenty-four hours. His dinner meeting with Jeff Heinz had gone very well–better than expected–but also introduced doubts about his beliefs regarding the war. The meeting with Theo Forrester had not been as productive, yet had accomplished a couple of potentially important things: He had viewed Charles Hunt, and he knew he had a reliable friend in Theo Forrester.

Rob still had plenty of time before dusk to accomplish a few more things. He found a nearby livery stable where he was able to hire a horse for a three-day minimum plus deposit. He had decided that he wanted to arrive early to Helms Grove in order to observe others as they arrived. This might also allow him to find a good hide and a good escape route. With that in mind, he opted for an early dinner, again eating alone, before returning to his room.

This time, as soon as he closed the door of his room, he went into action.

He removed his coat, tie, pistol, vest and shirt, leaving the thin cotton small shirt in place. Next he quickly opened his suitcase and removed the steel plate with straps that Pinkerton equipped him with. This would be worn to protect his chest and abdomen from gun shots or knives. He didn't know how effective it would be; certainly it would be better than nothing at all.

After cinching the plate's securing straps to his satisfaction, he put on his shirt and tie, followed by the vest and pistol. He viewed himself in the room's large dressing mirror, tilting the reflecting plate to take in the area of the vest where his pistol was hidden. He was amazed at how little bulge was there. He again put on his coat and returned to examine the effect. No one would ever know he was armed with a gun, unless, of course, he needed to use it.

The several practice draws that he did while in front of the mirror gave him the confidence to know that, if needed, the deadly little revolver could be brought quickly to hand. Rob also checked his boot knife, wanting the assurance of its availability when needed. This done, he placed his hat on his head and checked his overall appearance. Satisfied, he removed the hat once more to carry in hand until he was again outside.

Once out the door, he replaced the hat onto his head in practiced fashion, strode to the hitching rail and removed the reins. The horse was still saddled, which Rob re-checked to make secure before placing his boot in the stirrup and swinging his other leg over the seat. This was a tall, powerful horse well-suited to carrying a tall, powerful man. Together they made an impressive sight to anyone, especially pedestrians.

Without further delay, Rob rode this mount, Master by name, down the street according to the directions he had for finding Helms Grove. Several heads turned to get a better look at the large pair as they passed. He brought the horse to canter and then trotted for a while. This horse was well-trained, strong and tractable; he could not have asked for better. Dusk was some time off, but he wanted to be certain of his destination.

When he saw the bend in the road and the trees in the near distance matching the maître d's directions, Rob slowed the horse to a walk and focused all his attention on details as he approached the area. The land sloped slightly downhill away from the roadway as he left it to approach the woods. He estimated the area covered by mature trees to be no more than about ten acres and set about circling it in a counter-clockwise direction while looking for any special features. He found several things of interest.

There was a small stream running east-west which had slow-moving water flowing away from the woods. Its banks were gently sloped and afforded a good deal of concealment and cover as he followed the course of it into the grove. The water was shallow, only a foot or two deep. Rob was thinking it would provide a good getaway route should he need one. He wondered if it would serve as a hiding place while he waited for the meeting to convene. He rode Master along the bottom of the trench right at the water's edge, taking in what landmarks he could before it became too dark. Light would fade faster now as dusk approached.

He wished to do a more thorough job of scouting and was heading the horse up the bank and into the wooded area further north of where he had already been. Voices coming from further west and south announced the arrival of others into the grove. They had evidently entered the wood by following the same stream from where it intersected the road he had come in on. Rob used a calming voice and his hands to make certain Master wouldn't become spooked as he guided him cautiously in the direction of the men he had heard.

He reined to a halt about forty yards from the nearest edge of a sizable clearing on the opposite side of the stream from where he watched. The clearing, a rough circle, was probably thirty yards in diameter with a fire pit in the center. Several of the men already gathered were preparing to light a large collection of wood within a stone fire-ring. Between the gathering darkness as it fell and the added gloom of being under a forested canopy, it was difficult to make out details. Rob was happy for this bit of luck in his timing, as it meant they likely hadn't seen him either.

While considering when would be the right time to walk forward and show himself, he heard rustling in the undergrowth behind him. The question had answered itself ...

"Howdy, stranger. Something I kin help you with?" came the voice from behind.

Rob turned ever so slowly in the saddle, not wanting to give the wrong idea to anyone now watching. "Just come t' see what the meetin's about. Saw it in this mornin's paper." His reply was calm and easy, just as he'd hoped it would sound. His mind and heart were racing with the possibilities this moment might present.

The eyes of his inquirer met his own, locking briefly while they sized each other up. By his look, Rob could not see that the other man meant any particular trouble; just being cautious, he imagined.

"Always glad for new help in the cause, just can't be too careful. Whereabouts you from? You don't look familiar," came the follow-up question, to be expected under the circumstances.

"He's from Chicago, Bert. He's on our side and I'll vouch for him." This came from Jeff Heinz who had just reigned up on his horse. "His name's Rob Finn, an' he's already brought us more help than we could've expected. You'll hear about it soon enough." With that Jeff dismounted and signaled for Rob to do likewise. They then led their horses to a nearby horse picket line strung between the trees for that purpose. After tethering their horses, they shook one another's hands in greeting and turned toward the fire pit area. The others were starting to gather around it. "I'm a bit surprised to see you out here, away from town, Rob. I figured your business would keep you inside our fair city," Jeff tendered without recrimination.

"Hadn't planned t' attend, but, like I said, I saw the announcement in the paper. Decided t' see for myself what goes on. My patron expects thorough reports." Rob found it easy to act in an honest manner when his personal motives matched the script. "Kinda surprised seein' ya here, too, Jeff. Though I guess I shouldn't be."

About then, a tall, slender man dressed in black, having grey hair and beard piped up with, "Let's get the meetin' started. Won't be a formal lodge meetin'; we've got a couple o' visitors with us. But we can introduce the newcomers an' then get on t' some business. Guests give us yer first an' last name. Regulars–first names only. My name's Everett. Mr. Finn, since Jeff's already given us yer name, why don't ya tell us a little about yersel'?"

Which Rob did, keeping his cover story simple and short. The other newcomers introduced themselves by name and also told a little about themselves. Including Rob, there were seven visitors in all. There were more than twenty regular attendees. Rob couldn't get all the names, but he knew there were either twenty-three or twenty-four of them.

The business of the meeting included Jeff's report of the huge donation by Rob's patron and the fact that the sums had already been deposited in St. Louis area banks known by the group to have secret allegiances to the KGC organization. Many of those gathered, both visitors and regulars, looked at Rob with new respect. The business of the group progressed as they discussed how best to distribute the new funds and for what purposes. Everett, who Rob found out later to be a nephew or cousin of Charles Hunt, brought up a planned action that was soon to take place in Kentucky.

The Southern sympathizers were yet licking their wounds over the heavy Union victory at Vicksburg, Mississippi, and this fact came forth as Everett explained one of the needs for troops and funding. "General Kirby Smith is closing in on the Federals in Lexington. That man is as good as any we've got, an' we need to show these aggressors that we mean to end this thing. If we get General Smith enough men and equipment, we kin do jes that!"

No dates nor exact locations for this upcoming battle were mentioned. But the two things Rob noted with certainty based upon the passion and behavior of those leading this group: It would be soon and they were deadly earnest in their commitment to help the Rebel forces. These details were now locked in his memory, as he wondered how many other "Helms Grove" meetings were taking place in the Western theatre of the war that very night. This did not seem like some disconnected, renegade group to him.

There was very little more business to conduct, and that was of a local nature. The newcomers were not allowed to vote since they were not yet members, 'brothers' as they referred to one another. They were all invited to return for the next meeting. They were told that, if they had sponsors, they would be able to join the organization officially at that meeting, or possibly the one after. With that, the gathering broke up for the evening.

Everything had been peaceful without any immediate danger popping up.

Back at the picket rope, Rob and Jeff untied their horses, mounted and rode off toward the roadway together. They conversed about the details of the meeting as they rode.

"What'd'ja think?" Asked Jeff as soon as the two riders were a little ways from other ears. "Anything like your lodge in Chicago?"

"Oh, I'm no Knight of the KGC, Jeff. Not yet, anyhow." Rob's short answer betrayed no disdain for that group; he was merely stating the truth. Though he knew a few passwords and signs, using them in a setting where he could be easily discovered was to be avoided, except as a last resort. He had decided not to pretend membership in the split second in the grove when he'd been caught spying, in effect. Once that card was played, he couldn't recall it to his hand. It had been fortunate for him that he had not pretended otherwise–he'd have been too easily found out. This was not the same as an informal group meeting in the confines of Camp Douglas, where they eschewed the actual ritual practices of their organization. Had he pretended membership and the Helms Grove meeting decided to proceed in their formal ritual, he would have been found out.

"I was wonderin' if it would make sense for me t' join the lodge here, Jeff," he mentioned casually as he thought aloud. "It may be that I'll be spending quite a bit o' time in the area on business."

"Let me give that some thought, Rob. I'd be glad to sponsor you. It's just we need to think about what may be best for the Knights and what would be best for you. Where else do your business affairs take you?" An innocent enough question, especially given the conversation.

"In addition t' Chicago an' St. Louis, the boss mentioned sending me t' Indianapolis an' Louisville, though I haven't been t' either yet."

Jeff thought for a few moments before revealing his internal reflection, "Louisville, eh? That could make for some interesting possibilities."

They rode on in silence until they reached the city proper. They parted at an intersection just a couple of blocks from Rob's hotel. Inside the safety of his room, he was only too happy to remove the cumbersome and hot steel plate he had been wearing. It had offered him comforting protection. Still, it would be difficult to wear for longer periods.

* * * *

*6:00 a.m., Thursday, August 7th, 1862*
*Guest Room 207, Planters Hotel, St. Louis, Missouri*

A message had been slipped under the door of his room during the night. He saw it while preparing to dress for the day. It appeared to be from Jeff Heinz and merely said, "Meet for breakfast," in a man's block printing. It was signed "J.H."

Rob hurried his morning routine, not knowing what time he would be expected. When he arrived in the dining room, he learned he had nothing to fear; Jeff was seated across the room from the entry, waiting eagerly for his arrival. Rob signaled the maître d', and went straight across to seat himself at the table. A small urn and coffee service for two was already set out.

They again spoke in hushed tones while they drank coffee, ordered and ate their breakfast. Though Jeff seemed a little bit flushed in the face, Rob attributed that to the excitement his companion obviously felt over the news he had to share.

"Charles Hunt contacted my father last night before I returned from the Grove," Jeff began. "Evidently the news of your patron's generous donation got the old boy pretty excited. My father was very agitated as well; they'd both like to meet you before you return to Chicago, if that's at all going to be possible, Rob?" Though expressed as a question, it also carried a great deal of expectancy. How could he refuse this?

While he gave himself time to think a little longer, Rob replied tentatively with, "Hmmm. I was hoping t' catch a noon-time train back t' Chicago. Do ya think we could meet with 'em soon enough that I wouldn't have t' miss it?" He was actually hoping to miss meeting Hunt entirely on this trip, for fear the man might recognize him from the waiting area in Forrester's office. Upon reflection, he decided it didn't matter–his cover would hold up to this bit of scrutiny. He followed with by encouraging, "Can ya arrange it?"

"I believe I can, Rob," grinned Jeff. "Perhaps right here in the hotel." He turned on his heel to find the concierge, with whom he had a few words before handing the man a coin.

# CHAPTER SEVEN

# Chicago Conflicts

*8:00 a.m., Friday, August 8th, 1862*
*The Pinkerton Agency, Chicago, Illinois*

Allan Pinkerton was waiting for Rob the moment he came through the outer door of the agency's offices. Rob had hoped to have a few moments to share privately with Molly before the boss wanted his report. That was not to be, however.

Pinkerton escorted him briskly into his private office and offered him a seat as the man himself sat behind the desk. He was fairly bustling with enthusiasm–a state in which Rob could not recall ever seeing him before this. "What news, Longshot?! Yer wire didn't say much!"

Rob went over the details of his assignment to St. Louis, starting with his Tuesday afternoon meeting with Jeff Heinz. He covered the brief time he had spent with Theo Forrester and then the episode in Helms Grove and the ride back. Pinkerton interrupted at that point wanting to know as much detail as Rob could provide about the planned action in Kentucky. Since he had no more to share than what he had provided already, Rob did pause for a moment to add his own reflection upon a  small fact.

At dinner Tuesday evening, Jeff had mentioned a General Smith and something to do with Kentucky. Jeff's knowing of it in advance, and then the excitement within the group when Everett pitched the outline of the plan during their business meeting in the Grove confirmed the event's importance. The meetings at breakfast and after on Thursday morning added to that effect. Jeff, his father, and Charles Hunt all had looked solemnly delighted at the prospect of now being able to "Turn the tables on that tyrant, Lincoln, and his cronies." This had been the pronouncement coming from Hunt as they ended their brief get-together at the tail end of breakfast the day before. That trio had wanted Rob to convey to his anonymous patron their gratefulness at being able to deliver such a blow to their enemies. They wanted to thank him for his part in making the current plot possible.

In effect, Rob had just thanked the provider of the funds for the planned KGC-supported operation in Kentucky. Those who'd asked him to do so had no idea that the funds had originated with the Federal Government, the very one they hoped to defeat, as a way of baiting them into a trap. Rob was well aware of this fact, of course. He was feeling somewhat unsettled about his part in it. That was about to change.

Allan Pinkerton confided that they'd verified Kirby Smith's whereabouts and his rumored assignment to confront the Union troops amassing in central Kentucky from other sources.

He went on to say that there was growing concern among the Union generals that, given enough troops and supplies, Smith might be all but unstoppable in the upcoming campaign.

Pinkerton started his next sentence using the old nickname that he'd used earlier in this morning's meeting. Rob couldn't help but notice–it'd been a couple of months since Pinkerton had called him by it.

"Longshot," began the agency owner, "much as I hate to do so, I think it's time to bring that Sharps rifle out of retirement. This war could be over in an instant were the right general officer to be removed from the field of battle at the right time." He stared intently at Rob, watching for the big Irishman's reaction to this tack.

Rob returned the gaze with equal steadiness and intensity. "What exactly do ya have in mind, sir? I thought we'd agreed I'd be done with that kind o' assignment."

"Don't I know it, lad. An' if there were another way, we'd try that first. But we'll only get one chance at this; one shot. We can't afford not to take it, nor to miss. Kirby Smith is as capable a general as the South has ever produced. If he were to meet our Union forces on the field with an equal or greater force, there'd be hell to pay. An' that's the fact." With that, Pinkerton rapped his knuckles on his desk for emphasis. "It's not just me asking ya, ordering ya to do this one last job with the rifle. The President himself suggested that ya to be the man to handle it. Kentucky's that important to him."

Rob paused to consider these latest words of the agency head. He considered his duty to his government, his agency and his family. He considered his own conscience and the deepening tide of guilt he carried therein. Lastly he considered some of his own recent reflections upon the rightness of war and its orders to assassinate enemies of the State. His doubt and confusions welled up in his brain in a wave of muddled, angry thoughts.

"Don't know if I can do it anymore, sir. It's been a long while, an' I'm not the same man I was then." His defense and explanation sounded weak in his own ears.

Pinkerton continued looking at Rob. After a moment he continued, "I believe y t' be sincere, Longshot, and I haven't forgotten our agreement. I wish there was some other way, some other agent we could send. Plain fact of the matter is, there isn't. Ye'r our best hope for eliminating this threat to the Union. I know it's a heavy request an' a tough assignment. But I've got to ask ya this one last time. We need yer skill now, Rob, like never before. Y've got a couple days before y'll need to leave. Why not rest up a while? Then in a couple of days, say Wednesday of next week, if ya still feel the same way, come in an' we'll talk about it. What'dya say to that?"

Feeling defeated at again being asked to assassinate another human being, and disappointed after having been told he wouldn't be needed in this way again, Rob managed to mumble words to the effect that he would return on Wednesday no matter what. Meanwhile, he planned to stop in the outer office to see how Molly was getting along without her brother, then to visit his family in Darien.

Rob shared these last two notions with his employer as he rose to leave the man's office.

"Good idea, Longshot. Why not do that? Take the time ya have comin', an' take care of yer family. Who knows but these things'll sort themselves out by next Wednesday." With that he bade Rob farewell, returning to the paperwork on his desk.

Rob caught Molly's eye as he exited Pinkerton's office into the outer area of the agency. She signaled him to come over to her desk, which he gladly did. She smiled widely as he approached. He again noticed her attractiveness. Her dark hair and eyes were very different from Bridget's, or Maggie's or Cath's, for that matter, the other women closest in his life.

"How did things go in St. Louis, Rob?" asked Molly. She was happy to see him again, even though they'd only been apart for a matter of days.

"Well enough, judgin' by Mr. Pink's reaction," Rob answered. "How're ya gettin' along, Molly?" His care and concern for her were genuine enough; he just was not convinced he was deserving to pursue such a fine younger woman. Molly was employed, capable, and pretty. She would certainly still have plenty of prospects without a forty-two-year-old widower with children joining that queue. All that aside, he enjoyed her company and knew he was falling in love with her.

Molly's countenance altered slightly as she took in his question. There was a moment of sadness that passed across her pretty face, followed by a flash of thoughtfulness before she replied lightly, "I'm fine, Rob. Are you in the city for the next few days? I'd like you to come around for dinner, if you have the time."

Under other circumstances, Rob would have snapped up her offer like a starving man going after food. He had been steeling himself against just such a temptation, knowing that he really needed to be home with his children again, and without delay.

"Oh, Molly! If only I could. But I've not seen the wee ones since I left Darien a month back. I need t' see how they're gettin' on without me." Rob paused, straining within himself at the conflict of having to refuse her offer. Then he charged ahead with what he'd been thinking about. "Will ya care t' join me for a train ride home, an' meet the family?" His face beamed forth the smile reflecting the joy of his words as he asked. "We kin put ya up–no trouble, for the day or two y'd be stayin'. Y'll have a room t' yersel', an' so I'll be stayin' wi' th' neighbors, so I will!" When he got excited he dropped consonants as though made of mercury.

Disappointment washed across Molly's face now, replacing the earlier look of hope there just moments earlier as she'd tendered her offer of dinner to Rob. "I can't be absent from work just now, Rob. Mr. Pinkerton would never allow it with everything that's goin' on. I'd love to, but I just can't." She seemed sadly resigned to the situation.

"Maybe I can fix it with Mr. Pink," Rob brightened. "How about if ya work a half day tomorrow an' we have ya back by Monday afternoon? I'll even come back a day early, on Tuesday instead of Wednesday. How kin he say no t' that?" His enthusiasm was contagious and Molly's lit-up smile reflected his own. He was back down the aisle toward the private office before she could object further.

When Rob returned only a few moments later, his smile announced the success of his quest before his words did.

"Molly, just say 'yes', an' it's all arranged. Yer ticket'll be waitin' wi' th' agent at th' station. I'll leave today so everything'll be ready for ya. Y'll be with us for Saturday dinner, an' all day Sunday. Then Monday after breakfast yer back on the train. I'll be right after ya on Tuesday t' lend a hand in the office. What'll ya say now, lass?"

Laughing at his delivery, she replied, "Well, I can't say no t' all o' that, now can I?"

"Good! Then it's settled. The ticket'll be in yer own name. Don't be late, ya know. They don't hold that train. Not even fer pretty young Scottish lassies." His wink and smile won her heart in that moment. And it was a very good heart, at that. Looking over at the grandfather clock alongside the entryway of the office he exclaimed, "Oh me! Look at the time! I must go or be late mysel'!" With that, the now-energized Rob took leave of his co-workers, including Molly, with a wave as he took his hat with him out the door. A moment later he was back looking at Molly with a twinkle in his eye. "See ya tomorrah, Molly. We'll meet ya at the train station in Darien!" When he left this time he was heard whistling as he strode down the hallway and out the door of the building. His concerns about using his rifle on the job again had vanished for the time being.

Rob's happy mood carried him back to his sleeping room, where he gathered up his things, and on into the train station, where he purchased his round-trip ticket, as well as one for Molly. He grabbed a quick bite to eat at one of the eateries in the station and boarded the train with ten minutes to spare. He was surprised several times since leaving the office to hear himself whistling. He could not recall the last time he had whistled. As he sat waiting for the train to leave the station, Rob idly wondered at the title of the tune he had been whistling and humming over and over to himself, "Sleeping, I dreamed love."

\* \* \* \*

It was growing dark when he stepped off the train in Darien. The cause of his late arrival had been greater-than-usual delays in changing trains between the Chicago & Northwestern Railroad and the Racine & Mississippi Railway. He had not wired ahead to his family, so no one was expecting him and he privately enjoyed his solitary walk down the main street of the little town as he headed to his home. Before reaching it, he could see lights on behind the curtains in the window. Rob wondered if the children would be in bed. He decided to see how things went. Even though it was his own home, he had already decided not to just barge in, possibly frightening whoever was still awake. Instead he gently knocked while standing in the doorway on the wooden porch.

Maggie nearly fainted upon opening the door and seeing the tall, handsome man. He was still dressed in his fancy suit clothes which had been his working outfit while on assignment in St. Louis. He hadn't thought to change before leaving Chicago. In this little rural community, Rob was known as a farmer. His normal attire would be the clothes of a farmer. His family had never seen him in business clothing and had only seen pictures of him in his soldier's uniform. The shock was understandable.

So a surprised Maggie peered out the door at him, followed by Cath who leaned around to catch a look at what had so frozen Maggie in place. Cath's greeting was a shriek that brought the other children up from their beds, who had just been put to bed a few minutes before and were not yet asleep. As the younger ones emerged from their sleeping rooms, Maggie and Cath were just peeling themselves off from giving Rob a huge welcoming hug. He knelt down to embrace the three remaining children: Mary, John and Robert. Mary and John had each come forth in turn. The surviving twin, Robert, had to be brought to his father for the greeting by Cath. Robert was not yet three, and was wary of the huge man before him–a man that the little boy barely knew.

By quiet words and subtle signals, Maggie and Cath let the other three children know they would be allowed to stay up to honor their father's homecoming. But as soon as the yawns and drooping eyes started becoming frequent, the two caregivers ushered them back to their beds. They went willingly enough.

Rob was seated at the table as he took in this wonderful, domestic scene. He could not miss the difference in both the young women. Maggie was filling out, as was Catherine. Could she even be called a girl any longer? Did she still go by Cath? He had a momentary twinge of sadness that Bridget was gone; never again able to enjoy their children as they grew up. But the sorrow passed quickly now. That was yesterday's burden. He cherished Bridget's memory but would not be dragged down by sorrow. As he looked up into into the faces of the two others still present in the room with him, he saw Catherine's wide smile of welcome and relief. What he saw on Maggie's young face and in her eyes was neither easy to describe nor even acknowledge. She was not half his age.

He was reminded that he had yet to tell them of the impending visit for tomorrow, yet was in no rush to blurt out such a matter. He decided to let things take their course for a while. "So then, what's all the news in Darien, ladies?" Rob asked, smiling slightly, addressing the two young women as equals.

They responded, in turns, with various tellings of births, a wedding, a small fire at Duffy's mill and then, lastly and sadly, more deaths to report from the cholera that had lingered for weeks earlier that year, gathering its grim harvest. Fortunately the sweep had ended shortly after Rob had left, with only nine more local residents in the west end of the county succumbing. As bad as that was, all of them were grateful it had not been worse, especially under this one roof.

They exchanged small talk for a little while longer, the girls asking Rob about his work and his part in the war. Rob avoiding mention of what he'd actually been up to. He did say that most of his work lately had been in offices and cities. He also mentioned he would probably be away on a longer assignment starting the following week. Neither of them complained. They merely expressed their wishes that he could stay longer.

It would not do to drag out the telling of his other news. Rob had no desire to make it onerous or distasteful. He decided to plunge ahead as though Maggie were merely his employee, the nanny for his children, which was the case. Her other designs upon him were pure fantasy, as far as he was concerned. He refused to consider a match between an eighteen-year-old girl and himself. It just wasn't right. So plunge ahead he did, opting to ignore Maggie's obvious designs on him.

"We're havin' a guest for dinner tomorrow, some one I know from my work for the Army," he started. Both the young women smiled and exchanged expectant glances between them. How exciting to have a visiting soldier for dinner! "She'll be spending tomorrow night an' Sunday night as well," he included quickly, to see how things would fall out. He didn't have long to wait.

As she rose up with her fists clenched, Rob and Cath could see the temper rise in Maggie's cheeks as well. "She'll be spending the night, will she?! Not with me under the same roof, she won't!" With that she was through into the bedroom she shared with Cath, the door of which slammed behind her.

Looking toward Cath for some reassurance and understanding, Rob found only disbelief on her face. "Whatever in the worl' are ya thinkin' now, Rob Finn? Did ya give a thought to a single word afore sayin' it?" She stomped about for a time, straightening things that needed no straightening as she continued, "Father, do ya not care about that poor girl at all?"

Rob knew at once that Cath was right, he had been clumsy in delivering his news and had ill-regarded his young housekeeper's feelings. He had put them off as being unrealistic and fanciful. Now, upon seeing the effect of his words, he realized too late that Maggie's feelings were her own and, though awkward, were genuine. He'd made a real mess of his own homecoming visit. How in the world did things get so complicated? How did good intentions end up so wrong?

"Of course I care about her, about Maggie," he blurted in his own defense. "This family could not be gettin' by without her." As soon as the words left his mouth he was convinced of their truth. But Cath was on a mission and needed to drive home her point.

"Maybe ya'd best be thinkin' o' that then, afore ya go announcin' yer glorious schemes t' have overnight lady guests, don't ya think?" This was delivered by an incredulous Cath, hands on her hips. Her disbelief was nearly tangible.

"Now what?" asked Rob. He was plainly helpless when it came to extricating himself from this mess he had unwittingly created. "How do I apologize for hurtin' her feelings? How do I make this right?"

"Men!" was the most Cath could manage to get out before letting off a shallow shrug and shaking her head as she left Rob to himself in the main room of the house. She went into the bedroom that Maggie had entered minutes before and closed the door behind herself.

Rob turned down the lamps and retired to his bedroom, the one he had shared with Bridget. He removed his boots, pants and shirt and then sprawled diagonally across the bed. He doubted he would sleep much that night with all the problems he had to solve by morning.

* * *

*Early Saturday Morning, August 9th, 1862*
*The Finn family home, Darien, Wisconsin*

The sun pouring through the window curtains hit his eyes only a few moments later–or so it seemed. Rob could not believe it was morning.

He could hear the sounds of breakfast preparation coming through the door from the kitchen. He could also smell coffee. Among his favorite things about their small house was the outside entrance to his bedroom. He could dash out to the back house without meeting anyone in the common areas of the house.

Unless they happened to meet between the main house and the back house. Which is where he met Maggie this morning, of all mornings. Her eyes were a little red and puffy. He did not comment on this as he offered a cheery, "Good mornin', Maggie," as they passed one another on the little pathway.

"Good day to you, Mr. Finn," came the terse reply as she continued her return to the kitchen door. That didn't sound too good, thought Rob. But Maggie had spoken to him. And she had not run off, at the very least. So that was something positive. He hoped. With all his heart.

When he returned inside, he found the table laid for a hearty breakfast, a freshly-poured cup of coffee at his place, and all his children seated around the table, beaming smiles at their father. Except for Robert, who was regarding Rob with a worried expression that only those of his tender years can manage. Cath was managing Robert, who was often called Robbie, or even Rob in his father's absence, by having him seated on a small wooden crate whose design had been modified for the purpose. Maggie was no where to be seen; he noticed the door to her bedroom was closed.

Good morning greetings were passed all around and the children ate and picked at their food as children will. Rob dove right in after the bacon and eggs and toast before him. He looked at Cath, who seemed to regard him with some growing degree of wonder, finished chewing and swallowing a large mouthful of coffee before asking, "Where's Maggie?"

"Said she figured breakfast was just for real family members," answered Cath evenly. "Says that no one has t' tell her her place around here twice." The smugness of the delivery was profound.

"Oh, good God, " Rob muttered under his breath. "When will I ever learn." With that little self-admonition he shook his head. He finished his breakfast quickly, got up from the table and retrieved his traveling valise from alongside the door, where he had left it upon arrival the night before. He set the large leather bag, (this was the new one, provided by Pinkerton), on his chair while the younger children watched in amazement. He opened it and retrieved a paper-wrapped package from its ample interior.

The children's eyes widened when he went to the closed bedroom door, rapped on it with his knuckles, and announced, "Special delivery for the lady of this house, if you please." This was spoken formally, without any trace of his usual Irish brogue. He set the package carefully and gently on the floor just outside the door. He arranged the paper and bow to appear just so to anyone standing in that doorway.

Having accomplished all this, he took a couple steps back and waited with an expectant smile plastered on his large face. The result of this morning's social experiment was destined to take a little more time than the one he'd tried the night before.

It was not too long, however, before they could hear movement behind that door. The doorknob finally moved, slowly, and eventually the door opened a crack. Then it opened a little more. Then a little more, and a little more. Finally it was wide-open and Maggie stood there, mouth-open, staring at the package with its bow. In that moment she looked like a full-grown adult woman, alight with joy. And yet she was still an eighteen-year-old with a full life of her own ahead of her.

She advanced slowly into the tiny hallway and gingerly took the package in her hands. She felt it and raised it to her own eye level. She even gave it a little sniff. Finally, she looked at Rob, and with a very slight, very tentative smile, asked in a small voice, "Is this for me?"

"Straight from Barrett & King's in downtown Chicago, missy," he winked through his smiling eyes. "Just for you!" He held forth his arms in welcome, hoping she would take him up on his obvious offer for a hug. She did not disappoint, but rushed straight into his open arms as though they were the gates to heaven. Maggie blinked back tears of joy once she had stepped back from their happy embrace and held the package as though afraid to open it.

"Go ahead, Maggie. Open it. It really is for you." Rob's simple encouragement was all she needed.

The pretty wrapping paper was quickly shredded, much to the delight of the small children, who quickly claimed it all as their newest toy. What came forth was a surprise to all in the room, excepting Rob.

Maggie held the brightly colored dress against herself and she, as well as Cath, were amazed once more. It seemed it would fit her quite well.

"Well, Mr. Rob Finn, how in the world did you do that?" the exasperated young lady asked. "How did you get it made to my size?"

"It's all the fashion in the big cities these days," answered Rob. "It's called women's ready-to-wear clothing. There were several saleswomen in the store and one was about your size, or so I guessed. She said this would be the size she would wear. Do you like it?" His merriment was infectious to all of them. Even the youngest, Robert, was excited by the goings on.

"Rob, I love it!" Maggie's enthusiasm was genuine, which delighted Rob. He was hopeful that he was, or soon would be, forgiven his previous evening's indiscretion. But there was much more in his valise that he wanted to bring forth.

"Good," he responded. "I hope everyone will like their presents."

With that he brought forth a variety of gaily wrapped packages, one for each of his children. Maggie, of course, had her surprise first.

Cath and Maggie helped the younger children open their packages amidst gleeful shouts and sounds of every description. Mary got a pair of combs for her hair and a doll; John got a pair of trousers and a slingshot. Little Robert ended up with a large candy sucker on a stick, which pleased him just fine. Once these had all been opened and their new owners settled, it was Cath's turn.

She opened her package without further delay. "Oh, Daddy," she exclaimed. "This is too wonderful!" She was referring to her own ready-to-wear dress which, though different from the one for Maggie, still was very grown-up and beautifully colored. In addition, Rob had the store include a pair of dress shoes to be worn for church and special occasions. The shoe size had been a total guess, which he explained saying, "The saleslady suggested I get a pair that would be too big. That way you could stuff 'em with something for now, an' maybe grow into 'em later." Again, his exuberant hopefulness was contagious and they all laughed and hugged and laughed some more.

Even surrounded by this now joyful throng, Rob was acutely aware that time was passing quickly. He needed to complete his patching up of differences within the household and prepare for his guest. This time he was planning on being more gentle, more sensitive to Maggie's and Cath's feelings. He could learn, he told himself. He hoped he was right in that assertion. He had no desire to "escape the frying pan merely to land in the fire", as the saying went among the troops. He needed to get Molly's welcome and visit settled before he had another conflagration on his hands.

With that in mind, he suggested he help with the dishes. He knew the young women were not stupid–they would see through this plot of his, and so decided to turn it to best advantage. He was also a truthful person, so deciding to be up front with his motives was an easy matter.

"What say we discuss this evenin's' visitor while I help the two o' ya clean up?" he offered. "Before anyone's upset, let me tell ya a few things an' then ya kin ask all th' questions ya want. That alright wi' th' two o' ya'?"

Maggie and Cath both nodded "yes" to his question.

"Good. Then the first is her name: she's called Molly. An' before going further, you need t' know she's had a terrible loss, though we won't talk about it unless she brings it up. Her brother, John, who she loved very much an' who was my good friend, was killed in the line of duty just a month ago. I was there when he died. John was a good man, an' Molly's not over his death yet. She's a very nice lady, though lots older than th' two o' ya, an' I thought it would be nice for her t' get away from the city for a while. She lives in Chicago, and works for Mr. Pinkerton, same as me. I hope y'll like her. Now, what else would ya like t' know in addition t' any o' that?" he asked politely.

Maggie and Cath looked back and forth between each other. Small gulps and swallows could be seen, as could the slightest welling of tears in the corners of each pair of eyes at the kitchen sink. Rob knew that once they had the information he had just given them, their two young-woman hearts would not be able to mistreat Molly–they would at least be pleasant while meeting her, and would make an effort to get to know her. He knew his household to be made up of kind, caring people, especially these two women. He was counting on that right now.

They were nearly done drying and putting away everything from breakfast when Rob added, "I'll be staying either at the Morris place or with the McCanns, depending on who has room, so Molly'll be using my bedroom while she's here with us. I hope we can make her feel welcome." The last phrase was added with sincerity, even though he was certain the two young women were already way ahead of him. "Her train will be in this evenin', hopefully early–about four-thirty. I'm wonderin' if I should meet her alone, or would anyone else care t' join me?"

Again the two women looked at each other. They had learned to communicate silently in their tasks of caring for the house and younger children. There was a little flitting of the eyes before Cath nodded at Maggie. Maggie spoke their decision. "I'll meet Molly at the train with you, Rob. Cath'll look after the children here while we fetch Molly home. If that'll be all right with you, that is ..."

Rob was immensely relieved at the return of tranquility within his small home, so his heartfelt reply was, "That would be perfect, just perfect, ladies. Thanks t' the both o' ya."

# CHAPTER EIGHT

# Kentucky Bound

*Sunday, August 24th, 1862*
*On the railway south of Indianapolis, Indiana heading toward*
*Louisville, Kentucky*

As his rail conveyances bore him further south, Rob had
plenty of time to consider all the many things swirling around in
his world, and thus in his head at that time. Pinkerton had
wanted him to avoid all other contact on this mission and to
travel and operate in his Union uniform of a cavalry sergeant, the
thinking being that, since Kentucky was no longer officially neu-
tral, he would be able to travel about freely. He would also be on
horseback, once he got off the train.

Further thoughts were that anyone caught and charged
with spying at this stage of the war were in additional jeopardy;
both sides in the conflict were hanging accused spies–often on
very little evidence. Rob had best not be caught in civilian clothing while carrying out his mission goals. As always, he carried
special orders and warrants secreted about his person for use
should he become waylaid by overzealous members of the Union

forces. Union General William "Bull" Nelson had also been wired instructions to leave a certain sergeant unattached from his regiments. Rob carried a copy of this wire, as well.

In addition to those documents, he had his training and experience among the KGC organizations and might be able to bluff his way out of a tangle should that arise in the course of this mission. Again he would have to see how things unfolded in the field to plot each of his moves as events developed in sequence. The overall plan was for him to get in close to where the Confederate forces were gathering and then make a killing shot on the South's General Kirby Smith, before Smith could bring the Northern Army to battle. Once that was completed, he was to make his way back to Southern Illinois, or even as far as St. Louis, and resume his role as a Northern businessman sympathizing with the South. He would gather more information to further weaken the efforts of the Knights of the Golden Circle.

All of which would be fine, so long as he could enter the battle area, find a suitable hide and an escape route, then plan and make his shot. His moral considerations aside, it would still be a very difficult mission to accomplish. General officers who were running armies around a campaign area did not tend to stay in any spot for very long.

It was late; he guessed it must be near midnight. He could have checked his time piece, it just didn't really make any difference. Whenever he arrived would have to be time enough to do his job. He had just boarded the ferry that would take him into Louisville, where he would catch the final railroad leg of the journey. This one should take him into Lexington, where he hoped to report to a headquarters company, show his papers to the ranking officer, and draw a horse. From there he would find his own way to where the Rebel forces were bivouacked and start picking the sight for his attack. Assassination, as he now regarded it.

Rob settled in after stowing his gear. He didn't know how long he'd be on this train, but he thought it would be less than two hours. He thought back to his last few days in Darien and Chicago before he had gotten his final orders, money, clothing and other equipment.

Things had gotten fairly muddled around during his last three weeks in Darien and Chicago. Molly's visit to his home in Darien had gone far better than he'd had any right to expect. She got along well with Cath, and the younger children seemed to adore her. Molly seemed to return their adoration and spent time playing with and talking to each one of them. Maggie was cool yet polite. It was apparent they weren't on a course to become fast friends anytime soon. Nevertheless, it was unfortunate that her visit was so brief.

His own return to Chicago found him with new and greater responsibilities in the agency's office and structure. Rob was now actually the senior intelligence agent operating out of the Chicago office, a fact which he found astounding, even though no others seemed to think it so. Thus, in addition to doing more training of new hires, he was now processing internal agency memoranda and supervising others. His days flew by. In the evenings, after leaving the office he headed directly toward Molly's small home each day. After a hurried meal and some courtship talk during those visits, he would rush to his small hotel sleeping room to get a good night's rest before having to repeat the same process the next day. He was aware that Molly seemed to have a growing claim on him. Rob didn't mind; he felt he had a growing claim upon her as well. The thought was comforting in several ways.

On his last two days in the city, preparatory to leaving, he took the Sharps rifle over to the range at Camp Douglas and fired several rounds each day to assure himself, and Pinkerton, that his marksmanship skills were intact. In its own way, it was also a comfort to find that his abilities were still sharp, despite his growing reluctance to use them in the way he was ordered. Pinkerton had wanted to see the target papers from both Friday and Saturday upon his return. The man had let out a characteristic low whistle when he took the targets from Rob and looked at the holes in the papers. The targets had been set out at 300 yards, the longest distance available at the camp's range. All the bullet holes were touching one another, several overlapped. Almost to himself Pinkerton had said, "That's why I call ya Longshot."

Rob came back into the present moment when the train braked to a halt at a freight siding just north of Lexington, where he would be getting off. The Union forces had some camps already in place on the city's north side, and he was eager to make connections to complete his outfitting. As far as he was concerned, the sooner this mission was over, the sooner he would have some peace. He gathered his gear, shuffled through the mostly-empty car and climbed down the stair to the wooden platform.

Dawn wouldn't arrive for several hours yet, and he was plenty tired from more than a day's travel by rail. Changing trains frequently and being jostled about while riding aboard them did not lend itself to a restful experience. He was accustomed to being tired, though, and decided he could catch some sleep later in the day. According to the information he had, nothing would be occurring in the next week or so that would need his immediate attention. It is sometimes unthinkable how inaccurate military intelligence can be.

*  *  *  *

*Monday, August 25th, 1862*
*Lexington, Kentucky*

Looking every bit the part of a cavalry sergeant ready to report for duty, Rob hoisted his bedroll and knapsack onto his back and slung his heavy custom rifle over his shoulder before walking into the darkness away from the railroad tracks. He could hear, as well as smell, horses gathered not far in front of him and to his left. He followed his nose and ears to see if he might not discover a staging depot where he could requisition a good horse. The US Cavalry contracted only for black horses fourteen hands and over. Despite exacting standards calling for superior horses, not all the mounts in a depot were equal. Rob didn't care about color. For his purposes he needed a reliable horse: size, temperament and training were the qualities that mattered most. In theory, the horses available to him would already be screened and chosen for these traits.

He was in luck. It was indeed a corral of the US Cavalry depot whose sounds and smells had drawn him. What he needed to do now was find a suitable officer in charge to deal with, show some of his documentation and select a mount. While it was too dark to inspect horses, this was the US Army. He followed his nose to a open-ended tent with the aroma of burnt coffee surrounding it, expecting he would find the duty officer there.

He came to attention and saluted the young lieutenant and presented his warrant to draw a horse of his choosing, together with a blanket, saddle and tack. Rob himself did not know how Pinkerton had managed to get the signature of General Don Carlos Buell on these and other of his orders. The officer looked at the document, which Rob was not certain the youngster could actually read, and then pronounced, "Y'll haf 't wait fer th' major, sergeant. Can't do nuthin' about a horse til he gits here. Take a seat; grab some coffee, 'f ya like."

"Thank you, sir," replied Rob, sticking to his best pronunciation. "Would it be alright if I were to catch some sleep instead?"

"Suit yersel'. Plenty o' places to stretch out 'round the yard here." With that he picked up a small block of wood he had been whittling on and went back to carving.

Rob removed his bedroll and knapsack, arranging them so he could lean comfortably against a nearby tree to sleep. He placed the sling of his rifle around his body in such a way that the gun could lie across his lap and yet not be picked up by another. It was an expensive rifle.

Before drifting off to sleep, Rob mused that, of the uniformed soldiers he'd seen since traveling south of Indianapolis, none seemed well-educated nor well-trained. Their clothing and footgear were ill-fitting and military discipline was not up to the level he was familiar with. Not that it mattered much. Come morning he would gather what he needed, including information about where he might safely observe the rebel camps at a distance, and then be on his way. Sitting mostly upright, his sleep was fitful. When he woke to the rising sun he was aware of the aches in his lower back and neck. Sleeping while seated on the damp ground had not been easy on his body.

This somewhat rested, if stiffly moving, cavalry sergeant straightened his uniform and gear before ambling over to the tent where he'd talked with the young lieutenant a few hours earlier. That lieutenant was nowhere to be seen; in his place was a quartermaster sergeant and a major of the Cavalry. He again reported, coming to attention and saluting before presenting his orders. It was apparent that Rob was the only one of the three who had taken time to address his military appearance. This reminded him of his observations about local military conditions before he had drifted off to sleep earlier.

The quartermaster sergeant took the papers from him, read them carefully and then gave a start when he reached the signature. Handing them to his superior officer, he said, "Ya'd better see these, Major. Seems th' sergeant here is someone special." The man had not risen from his seat at the small field table.

Major Donovan took the papers from his sergeant casually and nodded toward Rob. "Stand easy, sergeant. We're not big on formality 'round here. Where ya from?" The question was appended as the major raised an eyebrow at the signature on the orders before looking squarely at Rob.

"I'm from Wisconsin, by way of Chicago, sir." His reply was truthful, yet did not invite further inquiry, which was his plan.

"Wisconsin, eh? What brings ya t' our part of Kentucky, exactly, Sergeant Finn?"

Rob felt the stirrings of uneasiness knocking around his insides, but remained calm as he tapped the barrel of his rifle and answered, "Got a job for the ol'girl here, sir. Not allowed to say who it is. I can say as it would help me a good deal if you could direct me to where the Reb headquarters camp might be; also how I might get to within about a thousand yards of 'em without bein' seen."

Both the quartermaster sergeant and the major looked suddenly more alert at his straightforward admission and request for their help. The major actually straightened his own uniform tunic and sat up a little taller before offering his reply.

"Within a thousand yards, ya say?" Donovan rubbed his chin. "That won't be easy. Lot o' open ground 'tween us an' them. Howd'ya feel about traveling at night?"

"Done it often enough b'fore, sir. Takes longer, 'specially in places not familiar. But if th' horse is up t' it, I think I kin manage." Rob had slipped into more everyday dialogue, not wanting to seem uppity with his benefactors.

"Sergeant Finn, we're gonna setcha up with the bes' horse we got. Big, strong, an' smart—not a better mount in th' herd. See if we don't. Sergeant Waters, bring that big son-of-a-bitch around for us, will ya. What's 'is name agin?"

"Bricks, sir. 'is name is Bricks. Trainer 'at brought 'im in said he calls 'im that 'cause he's so steady on 'is feet. Surefooted 'e is, sir." Rob couldn't be certain, but thought he'd seen just a glimmer of mischief cross the other sergeant's features.

"Let 'im take 'is pick of the saddles an' tack, too, sergeant," the major called after the two noncommissioned officers who were already among the horses, separating the designated mount, Bricks, from the others. "We want the best we got fer a man with a special mission," he concluded before turning back to his table.

"Treat 'im right, this horse'll take ya anywhere," offered the man called Waters confidentially. "Just look at the size o' th' bastard, will ya? Strong as 'n ox, 'e is."

That much was obvious to even a casual eye. Bricks was an impressively large, well-muscled gelding, almost better suited for heavy draft work than the saddle. His coat was shiny and he immediately responded well to Rob's hand. The horse seemed to be good around people.

"Well broke t' saddle, is he?" Rob's was an expected inquiry under such circumstances. Good pairing to the horse under him was often the difference of life and death for any rider on or near a battlefield. This could be especially true in Rob's upcoming mission. Matters could change from very quiet and peaceful one moment to pandemonium the next. He could ill-afford to have a panicky horse as his partner in this enterprise. Some horses flinched at the sound of gun fire–particularly cannon fire–which could prove fatal if it was not controllable.

"He'll respond well enough, so long's the rider knows how t' handle horses," was Waters' quick comeback. "We have the contractor's guarantee o' that." Again Rob saw what appeared to be almost child-like mischief on the other man's face.

Rob led the horse around the inside of the corral several times, watching, talking to the animal, pausing, poking, prodding, feeling different parts of the equine legs and feet. After a few minutes of such exercise he was satisfied that this was a very sound horse. The rest he would not find out until they'd spent some time together with Rob in the saddle in control of the big brute.

Waters then led the way into the large tack building which housed all the saddles, bridles and harness leather that the supply company had on hand. Rob was able to quickly find and trial fit everything he would need. Almost as an afterthought he took a cavalry saber down from a hook holding several, together with the mounting sheath that would tie to his McClellan saddle. Overall he was feeling that he had done very well getting the items and quality that he had wanted.

As they exited the building, Rob carried the gear over to where Bricks had been temporarily hitched and, starting with the US Cavalry blanket, proceeded to saddle and bridle his new mount. Before returning to his own duty station, Waters told Rob he would need to stop there to sign out for his new issue of horse, saddle, blanket, bridle, rifle scabbard, and sword. Rob knew this to be the way the Army operated and nodded his assent. When the quartermaster sergeant disappeared around the corner of the building, Rob idly wondered what kind of character the man really was; what did he do in civilian life before this war came along?

Bricks followed Rob's leading through the camp area to a hitching rail where Rob left him tied while attending to his remaining business with the major and side-kick sergeant. To his happy surprise, the major held forth a sheet of paper with some very well drawn-in details and labels.

"This is where y'll be wanting t' travel t' get t' the Rebs, Sergeant." Donovan pointed to the lower portion of the map in his hand. "I'm a surveyor by trade, an' I was working that whole area from Richmond 'n' south. Nice land. Couple o' small streams, not much marsh or bog. Gently rolling. Lots o' trees t' the edges o' this here valley." He again pointed to demonstrate the features as he described them. "Ya stay t' the west o' this low ridge here, ya should be alright. But y'll need t' go all the way south—nearly to Berea before y'll see 'em. They'll be stickin' t' the pike when they march north, so stay off the roads."

It appeared to be a good map and good advice, for which Rob was grateful. Feeling the good will for this helpful gesture arise within him, he commented that, "Stayin' off o' roads shouldn't be too hard fer this old farmer. Spent most o' my life in the fields."

"Farmer, eh?" remarked Waters, "Shoulda known. I was a storekeeper, ma'sel'." Waters seemed to regard his life's station before the war as being superior to those who worked the fields. Rob wondered if he had been an honest storekeeper but decided it best not to ask.

"Don't be forgettin' this is horse country, Sergeant Finn. Fences in the dark kin be mighty hard t' see. Ya don't want t' be runnin' in t'one." Donovan was again giving sound advice for traveling in the dark in an unknown territory. "Find a lane between two horse farms an' you can make good time. I've drawn in a good one down there below the ridge. It runs for several miles north an' south."

"Thank you, Major, much appreciated." Rob turned toward his horse. He didn't bother with a salute, nor coming to attention. Things were so informal in this camp it was more like a gathering of neighbors than a military post.

"Now we'll see what this big fella can do," Rob thought to himself as he untied and mounted Bricks. He was still in need of rest after his days of short sleep during his trip south, but the idea of riding for a while during daylight made sense while he was this far north of the enemy. He would still be alert and scouting as he rode. No point in being careless. Dining and sleeping in the Richmond area became his goal for the rest of that day. There should be plenty of time left to scout the territory south of Richmond. He had been told there was no way the Rebels would be ready to fight before the first week of September.

As he rode south on the nearly deserted roadway between Lexington and Richmond, Rob tried gently putting Bricks through his paces. The horse responded well and had an easy gait to ride whether walking, cantering or even trotting. Knowing there would be no better time to test him out, he urged the big horse into a gallop. His speed and power were wonderful and this horse was smooth as he ate up the road ahead of him. Rob gave him free rein for a little while, then finally slowed him to a lope, then a trot. By dusk they were walking into Richmond, ready to find food and shelter for the night.

They turned in at a local livery stable that showed light shining from within. He and the operator of the business quickly agreed on a price for stabling the horse, and also allowed Rob to sleep under the roof of the building. He was just too tired to seek better accommodations for himself that night.

# CHAPTER NINE

# Richmond And Big Hill

*Tuesday morning, August 26th, 1862*
*The city of Richmond, Kentucky*

Upon coming awake in the livery stable where he had spent the night, Rob felt more refreshed from his night's sleep than he had in many days. The combination of riding most of the previous day in fresh air and being able to stretch out on his bedroll placed over an abundant pallet of straw seemed to make all the difference. There was just a hint of soreness to his backside and the inside of his thighs which he knew to expect from not having been on a saddle horse much in the past several weeks. That, and Bricks' immense size had stretched some of Rob's muscles which had not been lately used.

He was tempted to luxuriate longer on the soft padding beneath him, but knowing he could not afford to, forced himself to rise and start his day. He fed some oats and hay to his horse and put fresh water into the trough. Then he set about taking in his own breakfast of hardtack and jerky. He smelled coffee and looked up to see the stable owner approaching him with a steaming cup of the brown elixir.

"Sleep well, Sergeant?" the man, whose name Rob had learned was Josiah during their conversation the night before, asked as he held the mug forward for Rob to take.

"Sure 'nuf, did, Josiah. Thanks. What's all the racket out there?" He asked, gesturing toward the open barn door through which they could see wagons and troops passing northwards through the small city.

"Seems General Nelson doesn't think much of our telegraph service here," replied Josiah. "Can't really blame him for that. It's out half the time. Rumor says he's moving his headquarters company back up t' Lexington. Says he can run a battle from there just fine, so long's he's got reliable communications available."

"Hmmm. Guess that makes some sense. Well, I need t' make tracks south. Gotta join up with my outfit on the way t' Berea, I think it is. Ya wouldn't happen t' know where the troops are bivouacked south o' here, would ya?"

"You'll be wanting to stay straight south–don't veer west toward Berea. You're liable to run into a bunch of Confederates over that way. The Federal troops are supposedly gathered up at the base of Big Hill–can't miss it, Sergeant. Say, what'd you say yer name was, again?"

"Finn. Rob Finn, Josiah. There should be some Indiana Cavalry companies I'm supposed t' meet up with. I'm sure they'll be right where you say. Thanks for the coffee," he added as he handed his empty cup back to the stable owner, "What d'I owe ya?"

"Nuthin'," Josiah waved off Rob's offer, "least I kin do for those o' you fightin' to preserve the country."

Once again Rob was struck by how people seemed to most often think that seceding from the Union was wrong and that, somehow, fighting would restore unity, or as it was referred to, the Union. He was still pondering his own thoughts when Josiah bid him good day and added a hope that Rob fare well in his military duties. "If he only knew," thought Rob to himself. "If he only knew."

With that he returned the farewell to Josiah and continued to saddle his horse and pack his gear. As he cinched the saddle girth snug to Bricks' barrel, he wondered if Donovan could have deliberately suggested that he head to Berea, into the Rebel camps. That made him wonder further if the map and directions would be reliable at all, whether Donovan didn't know what he was talking about, or, worse, deliberately wanted to put Rob or his mission into harm's way. Either way, he would need to keep his wits about him as he threaded his way south among the armies of both sides. He needed to avoid them all as much as possible, making contact only on his terms in order to obtain updated information. A couple of things about those two he had dealt with in Lexington didn't set quite right.

That would have to take care of itself, he decided. For now he needed to get down the road. Hoisting himself up into position just outside the doorway of the stable assured he wouldn't suffer an embarrassing and painful knock on the head. Once aboard the tall horse, he was able to see to the ends of town in both directions looking down the main north-south thorough-fare. It really wasn't a big city. Rob thought about sending a telegram to Pinkerton. Since he didn't have anything to report yet and since the service was reported to be spotty at best here in Richmond, he opted not to. He swung the horse to the south and began what he hoped would be the last leg of his last assassina-tion mission.

The horse and rider pair had only been on the road south about two-and-a-half hours when Rob spotted a sizable hill ris-ing in the distance ahead of him. He had been riding almost due south, so imagined it must be Big Hill that he'd been told of. Af-ter riding a short while longer, his keen vision spotted human activity on either side of the road at the base of the hill. Plainly he could see tents set up in the formation of company streets, as they were called, and he could see men with rifles on their shoul-ders marching about in a few places. Since the uniforms of the North and those of the South were often similarly colored, he was uncertain whose army he was observing without there being any flags present.

He slowed the big horse and walked into the woods along the west side of the pike. Keeping to the trees allowed him a degree of concealment while he continued his approach cautiously. He was about to rein in and dismount when he saw a small version of the US flag on a pole being carried out from behind one of the further tents. Relieved, he continued to advance, scanning constantly to make sure he was not spotted before he wanted to be.

Finally Rob dismounted and slowly walked Bricks through the trees and past the small encampment. He was just south of the post when he noticed that the land was already starting to rise to the crest of the high hill ahead of him. The pike on his left passed between the highest hill and the rising, forested slope of the west side. He halted completely while he thought about things.

The troops nearest him were Union infantry by all appearances. There was only one horse tethered in the camp which indicated only one officer present. A larger encampment with many more horses, tents and even a number of supply wagons was further off, across the road from the infantry. That was a cavalry camp, of that much he was certain. This was a very exposed outpost to Rob's way of thinking. Not many forces and no means of escape. If he were to continue his scouting expedition

to the south he might find himself similarly cut off, with this
bunch his only refuge. He decided he needed to get further from
the roadway and all these soldiers if he were to continue his mission. He took out the map that Donovan had given him and
studied it again, comparing it now to the features of the land before him.

Big Hill was there as it should be and the road and small
waterway were also accurately in their places. The narrow valley
opening to the south of him was similarly accurately represented.
Running southward, the trees on the western slope of the valley's
shallow rim seemed to offer him the best opportunity to continue
southward unseen. This was what Donovan had recommended.
He wondered how close that path would take him to the Rebel
troops near Berea. He had no way of knowing. He couldn't afford the time to get bogged down with an infantry company or
regiment of cavalry who'd been left behind as skirmishers against
a possible Rebel advance. He needed to see the Confederate camp
that was further south on the Kingston Pike, assuming there was
one to see. If General Kirby Smith were not at that camp, he
might travel along this route eventually.

It seemed to Rob that this plan of action had the best
chance of succeeding with the plot to assassinate the general,
given the scarcity of information he had received and how little
time he'd had to surveil the area. Having several more days to
scout around and observe movements on the road would cer-

tainly improve his chances. Though he did not relish the idea of assassinating another target, he had not let Pinkerton down in the past. He had successfully completed all such assignments thus far.

Confidence from those prior missions, and their outcomes, fueled his decision to press onward into the far side of the valley and continue south in order to locate the Confederates. Rob believed he could pick up the whereabouts of his quarry and complete his task, distasteful though it was.

He remained on foot for a couple hundred yards, until sufficient trees and undergrowth between him and the Union camp blocked any possibility of being seen from that direction. He then mounted Bricks again and, with deliberate slowness and precision, the two of them picked their way into and through the woods rimming the west side of the little valley. Rob paused their progress frequently to listen, and to watch for movements that might indicate danger. As the daylight faded on their journey they had covered another several miles south.

They halted for the night and made camp with no fire. And, since they stayed within the cover of the woods, the mosquitoes were fierce and merciless all through the night, making sleep elusive.

* * * *

Back in Lexington, Major Samuel Donovan and Quarter-master Sergeant Orville Waters had a few small, private laughs when recounting their dealings with that "big, dumb, Irish sergeant," which was how they thought of and referred to Rob after he'd left on Bricks. Neither would have addressed the big sergeant in that way to his face, as neither were especially courageous nor large themselves.

They saw their ruse of deceiving the man into thinking he would be safe riding into Berea as a great joke. And on that horse! The very thought of it brought a peal of laughter from each of them. Bricks was so named because, at the first sound of cannon fire he would rear-up on his hind legs and bolt, dumping his rider like a load of bricks. Why the Cavalry had kept the horse, instead of destroying it, was anybody's guess.

Orville Waters did not often wrestle with matters of conscience; if something worked in his favor, he went that way. His code of ethics applied equally to pilferage of his employer's retail stock as well as to manipulating those of his acquaintance who could be easily led.

Sam Donovan, the surveyor, had been an acquaintance of his since several years before the hostilities between North and South gained momentum. They had not been close, merely passing greetings as passersby on the street.

Then one evening about eighteen months ago, they had spotted each other at the first local meeting of the Knights of the

Golden Circle. Both had joined that very evening, realizing that this organization's goals and their own were identical. Due to timing more than talent, both rose quickly into leadership roles in that fledgling lodge. Working to advance the goal of their secret fellowship resulted in a closer friendship than would have been natural for these two, given their vastly different economic and social strata.

* * * *

Jesse Harkins, ever eager to be part of something "special", and having no regard for what those around him considered right and proper, was overjoyed when his friend, Quartermaster Sergeant Orville Waters, invited him and his younger brother, Jacob, to join the Knights of the Golden Circle Lodge in Lexington, Kentucky. Jesse had known Waters for several years as a result of spending time together drinking shots of bourbon whiskey in a tavern they both frequented.

Orville's work as shopkeeper in a local general store had yielded benefits in the past—Jesse could often afford the discount deals that were offered by his friend. These always took place off the store's premises, so Jesse was certain that the discounts were of Waters' own design, but what did that matter to him? A man with Jesse's limited employment prospects needed all the help he could get when it came to stretching his meager income.

Jesse had been born club-footed and was thus shunned by other children growing up. Walking with his limping, heaving gait was challenging enough; running was entirely out of the question. In adulthood he resorted to day labor, usually of the sort that other men avoided. He frequently cleaned horse stalls for pennies, milked neighbor's house cows, or did whatever cleaning or tidying folks would pay him for. Neither army in the current conflict would seriously regard an attempt on his part to enlist. He was effectively cast as a spectator in the great events that surrounded him. The same applied to his brother, Jacob, whom everyone called Jake.

Jake Harkins had been born with a hair-lip and cleft-palette; what sounds he uttered when trying to speak were unintelligible to all but Jesse and their mother. As a result of this speech impediment, most people believed that Jake was slow-witted. Sadly, this was true of Jake's overall condition–he was challenged mentally and had not the means to communicate readily with many other people. He was known on sight throughout those neighborhoods of Lexington adjacent to were the Harkins house stood. Jake was the tall, lanky dumb kid with a perpetual smile on his face.

He was gifted in his way with animals, possibly because of his mental condition. Jake was very patient with others, especially animals, and did not esteem himself too highly for any job. He cleaned outhouses and dug new ones and hauled away every type of vile refuse to the edge of town in his wheelbarrow. Though folks respected and appreciated the services Jake provided, they did not extend their liking to the young man himself. Other than his brother, he was a friendless soul.

Another consequence of Jake's oral and mental setbacks was that he was always willing to be a follower, especially of his brother, Jesse, whom he adored. Whatever else would be said of Jesse, he did genuinely care about and for his disadvantaged brother. Though Jesse often found Jake to be an annoyance, he seldom showed his pique and always protected his sibling from mistreatment by others. As a further consequence, their brothers' bond was exceptionally strong and Jake took his lead and his orders from Jesse unquestioningly.

Together, the Harkins brothers made a nearly perfect team for the current scheme of manipulation and mayhem that Donovan and Waters had in mind for them.

* * * *

When he learned of Orville Waters' enlistment and immediate elevation in rank to quartermaster sergeant in the US Army, Jesse was sure there had been something more to the story. He was proud to call the newly-minted quartermaster sergeant a friend; more privately he was jealous, knowing no such opportunity awaited him–ever. He'd been puzzled, at first, that the man joined the Northern Army. Everything he'd ever heard Waters say on the subject of the conflict was that, "'Em damned Northern assholes need t' be taught a lesson–leave the South alone!" It wasn't until later that Jesse learned of the KGC and the real reasons behind Waters being in the uniform of their enemies.

All of which contributed to his leaping at the opportunity that Orville's invitation represented: belonging to a special and secret group.

Though their mother would have objected to their becoming Knights of that order, had she known, the two young men were secretly delighted. They had taken the oath willingly and anxiously hoped that their chance to help the cause against the northern aggressors would soon arrive. As so often happens when people want something badly enough, their chance found them quickly.

After Rob had left Lexington saddled onto Bricks' enormous back, Orville Waters had hurriedly gone to the Harkins home. Fortunately for his and Donovan's plan, the brothers were both at home. Though he wore it sloppily enough, Waters was proud of his uniform and rank, and was aware it impressed civilians that he was a man of authority. Once he had the two brothers following behind him, he wasted no time getting back to the cavalry depot.

Jesse and Jake were paying rapt attention as Donovan explained his plan to trap and waylay the unsuspecting sergeant who had left less than two hours before. His plan called for absolute secrecy and obedience to his directions. Donovan had every confidence that, even dumb as they appeared to be, the Harkins boys would be able to pull off his scheme and would then not breathe a word of it to anyone. He and his phony career as a Union major depended upon it. But they needed to get started immediately.

It helped that Jesse had worked for a couple of months with a horse breeder south of Richmond–he was familiar with the countryside thereabout. Both the Harkinses could ride well enough, nothing fancy, but they could sit a horse for hours. Waters had already saddled and readied two mounts that would not be missed from the herd, though they should be adequate to the job ahead.

The plan was simple: it called for Jesse and Jake to ride on through the night and camp a little ways off the road south of Richmond. They should take turns standing watch while the other slept, thus keeping an eye out for their intended victim, a large Union cavalry sergeant on a huge black horse. Once spotted, they would follow him at a distance, awaiting their chance to ambush the man. They were to kill him on the spot of their attack.

Though he couldn't speak well enough for others to understand him, Jake understood English. His brother Jesse had taught him to hate Northerners and to love the Knights of the Golden Circle. Donovan and Waters were responsible for the Harkinses becoming members of this cherished fraternity. The disadvantaged brothers were beside themselves with glee at the prospect of killing the enemy sergeant. This was just like being real soldiers!

Major Donovan was strongly against giving them a gun for their task, so Waters provided them with a large camp ax and two bowie knives to complete the chore. Such everyday tools as these would arouse no suspicion before or after the deed was done. After a few final instructions and details, the assailants set off after their prey.

*** 

*4:30 a.m. Wednesday, August 27th, 1862*
*On a wooded slope south of Big Hill, west of the Richmond Road*

Bricks was stirring at his lead line, which Rob had deliberately kept short. He did not yet know this horse well and hadn't wanted to waste time looking for him in the morning. He wondered what had disturbed the horse, then remembered that the Union cavalry camp was only a few miles away. It might also be that the animal was smelling or hearing the very Confederates Rob was hoping to find.

By the time he had managed his morning toilet and munched on some hardtack, false dawn was lighting the eastern sky. Dawn would be along shortly, and he wanted to be ready to move at first light. He decided to affix his steel protective plate under his tunic. Most of his gear fit pretty well within his saddlebags, but the small plate seemed to chafe on the horse's flank. Besides which, his mission would be more dangerous from today forward, until its completion.

Rob placed the Sharps rifle in the leather scabbard and the cavalry saber on to the saddle. He had just finished strapping on the plate covering his abdomen and chest area and was replacing his uniform tunic when he sensed, more than saw or heard, movement behind him. He turned to face his attacker in time to receive a glancing ax blow to his chest. In addition to the loud clang made by the contact, the plate succeeded in partially deflecting the strike. Without regarding the heavy cut in his shoulder, he lunged forward with his right arm extended, catching the ax-wielder in the throat with his clenched fist. The man's windpipe collapsed with the impact and he went down, coughing and fighting for air.

A split second later, the second attacker stumbled coming from his crouch underneath Bricks, as he attempted to follow his brother's ax blow with a knife thrust. His blade went wide of its intended mark and gouged into Rob's left thigh just above the knee; a painful wound, though not immediately dangerous. At that same moment, a huge black hoof with a military horseshoe on it came down on the face of the man holding the knife. Jake's last thought in this world was one of surprise. He believed he and this horse were friends.

Blood flowed freely from Rob's right shoulder and the pain from that wound and his leg shot through him like tongues of fire. He knew the second man was dead; there would be no surviving a skull-crushing blow such as that. He turned back to the first attacker to find him nearly dead also. The man was still clutching at his throat as he completed his final thrashings in the leaves on the forest floor. Bricks stood only a few feet away, breathing heavily and watching Rob. The horse was wide-eyed and plainly spooked, but stood his ground.

Rob knew he needed to think clearly and act quickly before his own strength slipped away. He knew he was losing blood, but had no way of assessing his wounds accurately. The ax blade had taken him high on the shoulder, nearly into his neck, and sliced down into his bicep. The searing pain had already started to become numb and his arm and hand tingled. As Bricks was already saddled and bridled, he decided to mount up and ride for the cavalry camp he had passed yesterday evening.

Once astride his horse, he ripped several lengths of a shirt he had pulled off the first attacker, using his teeth and his left hand. These he packed into the gash in his upper body to stanch the blood flow.

They were nearly out of the woods when he heard the unmistakeable sounds of a large cavalry troop moving north. These were large battle regiments, not headquarters companies. This long, wide column was on the road below where he sat. He halted Bricks while they peered out at the stream of mounted soldiers complete with battle flags announcing their states of origin, and the large Stars and Bars. The infantry that was alongside the mounted troopers was a spirited lot. Though many were barefooted, they all marched with energy and pride. Rob knew that this army would quickly overwhelm what little resistance he had seen on the north side of Big Hill.

He also knew there was no way he could move forward without being detected and captured. He gently backed Bricks into the woods and then slowly moved off to a spot where they could wait undetected while the column passed by. Reckoning that would take over an hour, he dismounted and set about to make himself and his horse comfortable. He drank from his canteen and found a place to tie Bricks where he would have both water from a little spring and some browse.

Afraid that lying down might start his shoulder bleeding again, he placed himself sitting upright against a tree on his spread-out bedroll.

When he finally awoke, Rob was aware of two things: an unspeakable thirst and the fact that the sun was already setting in the West. He had slept the entire day through. Once he had drunk enough water to slake his thirst, he realized that his head was throbbing and that his shoulder was extremely stiff and sore, as was the wound by his knee. He did not feel feverish and he was neither too weak nor too sore to move, so he got himself up and took a few steps about.

He went over to check on Bricks and found the animal calmly standing where he'd been left, seeming no worse for having spent the day tethered in one place. Considering his own present condition, Rob counted himself fortunate to be as well off as he was. Had the steel armor not reduced and deflected the ax blow, he would probably not have survived the attack. Had Bricks not dispatched his second attacker, he would probably be in much worse shape right now. Yes, he had plenty to be thankful for after the scrape he'd been through.

But that was not to say that he was out of danger. He needed to find somewhere to clean his wounds thoroughly and to get water, food, and shelter for himself and Bricks. And he still had the mission of assassination to complete with the now increased challenge of avoiding capture. As his enemy and target were now between him and safety he would need to be doubly cautious.

*Thursday, August 28th, 1862*
*North and east of Big Hill, Kentucky*

Rob and Bricks had traveled through the night. After crossing the Richmond pike and continuing on to what he considered a safe distance into the woods and hills on the east side of the narrow valley, they slowly worked their way back north. Rob had used the many campfires he could see on the valley's floor to guide them away from contact. He knew there would be skirmishers and pickets well out from the main encampments of the army as it moved north; he pointed well beyond the distance he estimated such outliers would be positioned.

When morning broke, they were still free and undetected. Bricks had walked carefully and slowly in the dark, picking his footing skillfully even while Rob occasionally dozed in the saddle. He was a smart horse and had shown plenty of heart when it came to caring for his rider. Rob's trust in the big gelding was growing as they were together longer. He had given the horse his own head for the entire night's travel and had not regretted that decision once.

He thought about trying to successfully complete his mission of assassination. Could he locate General Kirby Smith, find a good hide and an adequate escape route? He finally had to admit that he was fooling himself to think so. In his current physical condition, and considering his lack of familiarity with and inadequate time to scout the geography, there was no way he could see to complete the mission. It would be best to get back north, while avoiding capture, and communicate what he had learned. It would be smarter to live to fight another day.

Once he had made his decision, his mind and conscience were much clearer. His wounds were still painful and worrisome, but he believed he could manage to escape safely by conserving his energy and taking his time. With that in mind, Rob and Bricks headed northward and a little further east. They crossed a small creek with clear water where they paused; both took long slow drinks to restore themselves. Rob carefully rinsed his tunic and rung it out, then rolled it in his bedroll. For now he would rather be seen as a civilian. Next he removed his steel armor and, doing a better job of wrapping it in his spare clothing, he packed it into the opposite saddle bag from where it had chafed Bricks. He ate his last hardtack biscuit while Bricks munched on the last of the grain ration Rob was carrying.

As final preparation before resuming their northward travels, Rob encouraged Bricks to drink again while he himself refilled his canteen with the sweet-tasting water. He also removed, rinsed and replaced his bandages and undershirt as best he could. He was relieved that there was no sign of infection yet and he suffered no feverishness. He completed these ministrations without starting either of his wounds to bleed again.

They'd not slept since the day before, but he was hoping to forego further rest until they reached Richmond so he could send a telegram to Pinkerton. He was about to swing his leg over the saddle when the sound of the first cannon shot reached them. Bricks' ears flattened against his head, his eyes flew wide open and he started to rear up in panic as a cry of alarm escaped his equine throat.

Rob had always had an Irishman's love for horses and the instinct that accompanied that emotion is probably what spared him further harm. Instead of reacting with a harsh word or a whip, he quickly draped his wounded huge right arm over the horse's neck and hugged tightly. At the same time he spoke calmly in steady deep tones, "Steady, boy, steady." He repeated the gentling phrase several times over. The horse, initially tense and attempting to pull up, back and away, gradually relaxed and steadied, which allowed Rob to complete mounting into the saddle.

The man could sense that the horse was yet uncertain, so he remained in place, continuing to sooth the beast with voice and hand. Sure enough, another cannon was fired, followed by another and another. Each time the big guns' roar reached them, Bricks tensed and started to rear up as though he would buck and bolt. Each time the huge rider hugged the black neck and firmly but gently spoke his calming phrase, all the while running a massive hand along the horse's jaw and cheek. By the seventh or eighth volley, Bricks was much calmer than he had ever been when loud noises assaulted his ears. The horse was learning to trust this man more than any he had ever known. Man and beast were forging an alliance that crossed the species barrier normally separating them.

Shortly thereafter came a break in the cannonading, which was from further south in the valley, near the base of Big Hill. Rob decided they would be better off further from that action and set out again north. When the sound of cannon next reached their ears it was from a greater distance. Bricks did not give the noise much notice, though he was still on high alert.

After a couple of miles Rob could hear the sound of galloping horses coming up the valley from behind. Bricks' ears were perked up and swiveling about as he strove to take in the sounds as well. Rob headed deeper into the woods edging the east slope of the valley to keep hidden from sight. Within a few minutes there was a troop of thirty or so cavalry accompanying an artillery battery of four cannon and their limbers, and eight large supply wagons, all making their best time possible to the North. The riders and drivers kept looking back over their shoulders as they urged their mounts and teams to keep their speed. None of the valley riders were looking east; they were definitely running for their lives. Besides which, Rob and Bricks were in deep enough cover to remain undetectable to the passing Union soldiers.

The passage northward by various-sized groups of cavalry and wagons occurred twice more before mid-afternoon. Shortly after the third of the groups passed, Rob saw them pull up and join what appeared to be the two earlier bunches. In all, he estimated there to be upwards of two regiments hastily setting up camp along the road. In the distance, Rob could make out the buildings of Richmond. He wondered if he could make it back to Josiah at the livery stable, and from there to the telegraph office before it closed for the day. There was very little cover to shield his movements and the valley had opened out into plain again.

They would now take their chances over the open ground. While Bricks was capable of great speed for short bursts. Rob preferred not to test his speed against pursuers, since he was not certain how well he could ride in a gallop with his injuries. He walked them out from the remaining screen of trees and undergrowth, keeping to the east side of the cleared land away from the roadway. They hadn't gone more than a mile when they encountered a fence blocking their path and extending east to west from the road to as far east as he could see.

He took his chances with the road here, being close to town and having hidden his uniform tunic out of sight. The US brand on Bricks' rump and a similar mark on his saddle and saddle bags would identify them readily enough to any near enough to detect those markings. Since he had documentation to explain his way out of just about any questioning he might run into, he was not worried about capture or incarceration by the Union troops. It was a matter of keeping his mission secret and being allowed to travel about unhindered. He turned northward on the road and kept as close to the east edge of it as possible.

Traveling in this fashion, they reached the edge of Richmond unmolested. Even when a couple of men in Federal Blue uniforms had obviously noticed the brand and saddle markings, they said nothing. Perhaps the sight of the oversized horse and rider discouraged further curiosity. The blood-stained shirt covering the large shoulder wound and torn trouser leg near his left knee were evidence of a recent conflict. Perhaps these also dissuaded casual observers from inquiring about Rob's business.

In any event, Bricks arrived at the livery stable, bearing an exhausted and disheveled Rob Finn on his back. Josiah had been watching up the street as the pair approached his establishment and recognized Bricks from a distance. He took the reins from Rob, helped him down and hitched the horse for him.

"What in the world happened to you, Sergeant?" the concerned stablekeeper burst out when he could see Rob's injuries up close, "You look a ..."

"Shhhh ...," Rob cut off the man's question by placing a finger over his own lips and whispering quietly, "Shhh ... Shhh. Not out here ... inside," before ducking into the opening on the street side of the building.

Once they were inside away from public scrutiny, Rob explained that he had been attacked by a pair of men who he had already figured out to have been following him. He had a suspicion about how they'd gotten on his trail but did not mention that. At this point it was only a hunch and he couldn't prove anything. He needed Josiah's help.

"Can the operator at the telegraph office be trusted with a confidential matter?" was Rob's first question for the local man. Josiah assured him that the operator was indeed trustworthy–it was the sporadic availability of the wire being live that was questionable. There were plenty of Confederate sympathizers in the vicinity and sabotage of the wire was a frequent occurrence. Since General Bull Nelson had relocated his headquarters to Lexington several days earlier however, the telegraph service had been uninterrupted.

"Is there a doctor in town that can keep his mouth shut an' knows his medicines?" Rob was not a lover of the medical profession of his day, but did not want to succumb to fever or infection if he could avoid it.

"That's a harder order to fill, Sergeant," replied Josiah thoughtfully. "I have an idea of where you might get better help for that matter than you would around here," he added, nodding at Rob's torn shirt and shoulder. "Em Shakers over at Pleasant Hill is known for their Christian charity. They also do good doctorin' and don't take sides in earthly quarrels like this here war. If you're lookin' to lay low fer a while that's where I'd be headed. Of course, Lexington is a lot closer, even has a hospital. But I got a hunch yer not lookin' fer city lights just now, not meanin' t' pry."

"Josiah, you're readin' me real well. Let me get a wire sent t' my superiors, an' then maybe we kin look into that Shaker group. Are they a Catholic bunch, d'ya think?" Rob asked.

"Oh no, nothin' like that," Josiah chuckled. "'Bout as far from Catholic as ya kin get, I reckon. But good an' honest people is what they're known for, an' being good neighbors t' those around 'em an' those as happen upon 'em. If we kin get ya there, they'll take good care of ya fer as long as yer needin' it."

At the telegraph office, the operator followed the instructions precisely when Rob handed him the coded message to be sent to the address 'PNKTN'. The message read:

**Bird unruffled. Hunter broken wing. Healing req'd. Await**

**further. RF**

What it meant was:

The target, Kirby Smith was unharmed. The hunter, Rob Finn, was wounded and out of action. He would wait in place until he received further orders.

The operator kept the office open an additional forty-five minutes past the posted closing time while Rob and Josiah waited for the return message. Traffic on the wires had been unusually heavy that afternoon which added to the delay. The message from the Pinkerton agency read:

**Bird unimportant. Advise place of healing. MF bd AP**

Rob had no trouble understanding the brief message. He had the operator key back his two word reply:

**Pleasant Hill**

... and then paid the man for his work, gathered up his receipts and left. He followed Josiah back to the livery stable. As they walked along, they spoke briefly about the local actions having to do with the war, particularly General Nelson's being in Lexington and the growing rumor that Confederate General Kirby Smith was rapidly approaching Richmond. Rob was glad to think his decision, reinforced by the newly received telegram, let him off the hook for the Kirby Smith assassination. He didn't share the reason for his happiness with his companion.

# CHAPTER TEN

# On To Pleasant Hill

*After breakfast, Friday, August 29th, 1862*
*Main Street of Richmond, Kentucky*

Parting from those who helped one along life's journey was always difficult, so when Rob said good-bye to Josiah it was with heartfelt goodwill. The man had looked out for him, sheltered him, gave him good advice and cared for him and his horse. He felt as though he'd made a lifelong friend with this man he had known for a matter of hours since meeting him four days earlier.

He had re-provisioned himself for the two-day trip to Pleasant Hill, having packed enough food and water, including grain for Bricks. He would water the big horse from casual sources he found along the road. The path, as described by Josiah, wound around considerably. The first leg of the journey would carry them back north, almost to Lexington. Rob was now clothed completely in civilian attire. Also, to help with his disguise, Josiah had provided an oversized saddle blanket, replacing the US Cavalry-issued-and-labeled one that Rob had been using. The new blanket covered the U of US in the brand on

Bricks' hindquarter. That left most of the S showing, which would easily be presumed to be a private branding. Some elbow grease and pumice stone removed nearly all the military markings from the saddle and saddle bags. A generous working-in of axle grease followed by saddle soap served to hide the recent work from all but the most interested onlookers. Rob planned to avoid all of those that he might cross paths with.

\* \* \* \*

As he rode along, Rob was again grateful for his deliverance from the attack upon his person, and for the unexpected friendship and help given by Josiah. He marveled at the twists of fate he had experienced in the last several months. His two young sons dying, followed immediately by their mother's death had been like hammer blows to his spirit. His recovery from those horrible events was progressing when his friend and co-worker, John Ferguson, had been killed right next to him, through a stupid misunderstanding in this stupid war. He, Rob, who had taken multiple lives in his role as an assassin, was spared not only in the Camp Douglas fiasco, but had thus far survived the most recent attempt to kill him.

Again he puzzled over what seemed in his mortal mind to be the frivolities of God.

The balance of the day's travel was uneventful, other than the distant thunder of canon fire coming from behind him in the afternoon. What he would not learn until later was that those were the opening sounds of the Battle of Richmond, which would last for two days and provide the Confederacy with one of its most important victories against the Union to date. It was certainly a significant outcome for Kentucky and the western theatre of the war. As it turned out, General Kirby Smith's brilliant application of strategy and tactics carried the day. The forces under his direct command routed the Union regiments and captured over five thousand of their soldiers in this one action.

Rob rode on, untroubled by the sounds of war to his rear. He knew there was nothing he could do about whatever was taking place back there. He was certain that the Union forces would again prevail. He hoped that his new friend, Josiah, would not be adversely affected by the nearby military action. What he could not have known was that Josiah was already dead, killed by an errant canonball that had been fired so as to bounce through the lines of the enemy. Josiah had not been very near the lines of battle; he had been called upon to deliver a pair of fresh horses from his stable to the Union headquarters company at the rear and west of the action. He had been completing that order when he was cut down.

Rob's path lead north until he crossed the bridge over the Kentucky River, and then turned westward on a small road that Josiah had described to him. This track followed along the river much of the way; he could see it most of the time and could go down to it for water should they need to do so.

Rob stopped that evening at a crossroads that was somewhat more than halfway to his destination. The landmarks that Josiah had described were clear enough that he had no doubts about being on the right path. Again his heart filled with gratitude toward the helpful and selfless man.

He camped on a level area with plenty of grass and an easily accessible little stream which ran down to and joined the big river nearby. The north-south road that crossed there was more traveled than the one he had come in on. The area where he had set up camp was obviously well-used for that purpose by travelers.

Two other parties of travelers pulled off the road to camp near the crossroads that evening. One was a family of civilians with a two-horse team pulling a wagon. This group included a husband and wife with two young children, a boy and a girl. They seemed a peaceable, shy, and quiet group.

The second group was made up of three rather rough-looking characters: dirty, loud, and foul-mouthed men. They showed no concern for anyone as they set about banging their gear carelessly and crashing around in the underbrush nearby. None of the three exhibited the least bit of modesty when it came to taking care of personal business or their colorful choices of language in the presence of the young family members sharing this clearing for an evening.

Rob stood and was about to walk over to the three ruffians for a word when one of their number glanced up and made eye contact with the big Irishman. The ruffian barked something indiscernible to his companions, who looked at Rob and then fell silent. That was the end of the unwanted noise from that quarter for the rest of the night.

* * *

*Saturday, August 30th, 1862*
*Campsite near the Kentucky River between Richmond and Pleasant Hill*

Rob felt he was probably pushing his luck, so he kept to himself entirely the remainder of that night. He woke early, rose and readied himself and Bricks as quickly and quietly as possible, setting out before eating or having any coffee. He could allow Bricks a few good mouthfuls of fresh, green grass along the way and could nibble on a biscuit or two as he rode along. Though he slept through the night, he wasn't feeling as refreshed as usual, but didn't think much of it. He'd been on edge at the crossroads due to the ill-behaved threesome that arrived last evening. He put it all out of his mind as he pondered his upcoming experience with a religious community.

About two hours on the road, sudden movement off to one side of the road startled Bricks, who then lurched slightly. Rob had not been paying close attention to his surroundings and when the horse's gait changed abruptly, he was thoroughly jostled in the saddle. He thrust his right hand, which had been resting loosely on his right thigh, forward to grasp the saddle's horn to brace himself. That motion, and its swiftness, tore open his shoulder wound, producing an unexpectedly excruciating pain. Along with an outflow of blood and suppuration, he caught the unmistakeable stench of abscessed or rotting flesh. Even though it seemed slight, he knew he was in trouble and did not have time to waste.

Kicking Bricks into the horse's characteristically gentle canter was easy–both had been meandering along at a sedate pace for several days. Bricks' response showed an eagerness for the exercise, and the horse's long legs and stride ate up the miles faster than any mount Rob could remember. He hoped both their strength would last until he reached the welcome that he had been told to expect upon reaching Pleasant Hill.

He had originally planned to arrive in mid-to-late afternoon. Owing to traveling at a canter for an unbelievable time and distance, he spotted the brick administration building shortly after noon. Rob was really feeling the effects of his growing fever; his vision was starting to blur, his skin was clammy, and he felt much hotter than the weather should have indicated. He had emptied his canteen and was suffering from thirst. Added to these, he could not recall clearly the last several miles of the trip. They had arrived none too soon.

Bricks halted gently before the stately two-story building without verbal or tactile command. The horse was stressed, blowing and wheezing to regain his wind. He was coated in sweat and foam, and shaking all over as he labored to get sufficient air into his huge lungs.

Helpful, eager hands seemed to appear from nowhere and everywhere. Firmly, gently, quickly and expertly they removed rider from steed and carried him indoors where he would be tended. Others slowly and soothingly led Bricks to a large stable area with ample shade, water and hay. As Josiah had promised, they had arrived at a place of peace, shelter, and recovery.

* * * *

*Early evening, Tuesday, September 2, 1862*
*Infirmary room, Pleasant Hill Shaker Community, Kentucky*

Rob was unconscious for the first three full days of his stay with the Pleasant Hill Shakers. Collapsing into the hands and arms that greeted him upon arrival, he was in fitful, feverish sleep from the moment he was laid into a clean bed that Saturday afternoon until the following Tuesday evening. His fever had broken twice during the ordeal and he had flitted close to con-

sciousness several times. During those brief flashes of wakeful-
ness, he had overheard snatches of conversations taking place.
As he was emerging back into a more normal state of awareness
Tuesday evening, he remembered some of these. He very dis-
tinctly knew he had heard the words "soldier" and "deserter" and
"sergeant" while he'd been mostly out of it. He wondered what
these religious people were planning to do with him, but chose to
let them bring up what topics they would.

The convalescent patient's eyelids batted open and then
stayed that way revealing a pair of clear, dark and intelligent orbs
looking out upon the world. These eyes were greeted by a kindly
and smiling pair of blue eyes set in a peaceful, pretty face of ap-
proximately his same age. Or so he guessed. The owner of those
eyes was blonde-haired, with a bonnet of sorts worn in such a
way that not much of her tawny adornment could be viewed.
She was entirely clad from neck to toe in a simple gray dress of
the most modest style Rob could remember seeing. Over this she
wore a simple white linen yoke over her shoulders and a white
linen apron tied about her waist.

As it became obvious to her that he was awake, or mostly
so, she rose gracefully from her seated position and leaned closer
to his face, all the while observing all aspects of his condition
with those same keen eyes.

"Welcome, guest." These were the first words Rob heard
spoken by one of the strange creatures known as Shakers. The

voice was soft yet clear, and the simple greeting was offered with what Rob felt was genuine welcome. Rob found himself feeling immediately at ease in his new surroundings. And thus he came to make acquaintance with Sister Barbara, who had been his primary caregiver during the preceding seventy-two hours.

"How long have I been here?" asked Rob, not knowing what answer to expect. "How's my horse?" He had now expressed his two most pressing concerns.

"You are with us three days almost exactly, Sergeant, and your horse is fine and healthy. Your clothing and personal things are in the cabinet there against the wall and your tools of war are under lock and key in the steward's office." This was spoken softly and with no apparent judgement. She had merely made two statements of simple facts. To these she added, "My name is Sister Barbara and I am happy to assist you during your stay with us."

Her next words, a question, were equally soft and plain, "Have you any need at this moment?"

He did a quick self-assessment and found, to his utter amazement, that he had no needs. There was no pain and no fever. He felt clean, was not thirsty and did not even need to empty his bladder. The realization that this woman, or someone, had attended to even his most private personal needs while he was unconscious, caused him a brief moment of embarrassment. The flush of that emotion passed over his face and as quickly was gone.

Turning to his right shoulder to investigate his injury, he found it and his upper arm to be bound snugly in clean white linen bandages. No blood, no foul odors and no soreness could be detected. He reached down with his left hand under the bed-clothes to gently probe the wound above his knee. He found that it was also bandaged and pain free. Lastly he put his left hand to his face and discovered that he was unshaven.

"I believe I owe someone here for saving my life," he put forth. "Would that be you?" came his simple query.

"We are but the agents and ministers of God's good grace, sir. We all owe our lives and health to His provision. I'll tell the eldress that you're awake and ready to meet with her, if you have no objection."

"I'd be grateful for a wee bite o' somethin' first, if it's handy?" Rob asked sheepishly. "I'm just noticin' that I'm a bit peckish."

"That will be no trouble at all," Sister Barbara answered, "We're glad to know your appetite has returned." She spoke to someone in the hall outside the room, and in very short order a young woman, similarly attired, carried in a small tray with a plate, bowl, fork, napkin, cup of milk and a fresh cut flower in a tiny vase.

After finishing his meal of bread, cheese and a bowl of steamed garden vegetables with herbs, spices and a small amount of chicken, Rob was feeling much renewed. Sister Barbara bade him follow her, which he gladly did. As they passed down the stairway from the upstairs hall, he noticed that the railing dividing the hallway above continued down the middle of the stairs. Sister Barbara indicated that he should remain on the side of the rail opposite that which she occupied. Though he did not know it at the time, it was Rob's first exposure to the Shaker practice of celibacy. The sexes were nearly always kept separated; this even applied to married people.

He didn't know what to expect in meeting with the eldress, but was looking forward to learning more about these people who, because of their faith, were willing to go to great lengths to care for a complete stranger.

The eldress, Sister Elizabeth as she called herself, though seated during his visit, appeared to be a tall, angular woman somewhat older than he; in her fifties he guessed. She had a bonnet identical to that which Sister Barbara and the other young woman wore; in place of the gray dress and white apron that they wore, Sister Elizabeth was clad in a modest black dress that covered her completely from neck to toe. Her hands were folded comfortably on the desk before her when he was ushered into her office. She made no move to rise, nor shake hands, but her gaze went immediately to his face. Her eyes sought out his to make contact in a most penetrating way.

"It is good to see your return to health," she stated, "and finally meet our guest who has caused us some speculation. Please sit so we can talk awhile." She gestured toward the simple, straight-backed chair before her.

Once seated, Rob could not help but notice how comfortable and sturdy was this basic piece of furniture.

"I am Sister Elizabeth, one of two eldresses of this community. By what name should we call you, sir?" She wasted no time.

"I'm Robert Finn, ma'am. Born in Ireland, come t' this country in 1845 an' settled on me own small farm in Wisconsin. Folks call me Rob, which suits me fine."

"Thank you, Rob. We're happy you've come to us. I have a few questions that I hope you will answer so we can best determine our future course together?" She paused with one eyebrow raised, while he nodded affirmatively. "For the purposes of identifying you and preserving your belongings, we were obliged to go through your things, including your saddlebags, clothing and boots. As you can imagine, we found your uniform jacket and your papers, as well as the guns, saber and knife you were carrying. We make no judgement about any of these things, merely we take note of them." Again she paused, obviously waiting to see if he would comment. When he did not, she continued.

"Our community practices pacifism. We do not fight, we do not kill, nor do we tolerate those among us to do so. Your weapons will remain locked away while you reside with us; they will be returned when you decide to leave, which you are free to do at any time. You are also free to stay with us and share our communal life while you recover more fully. We invite and encourage you to do so. If you are hiding from the military or other elements of the government, we can and do offer some degree of refuge to you. Our males are not required to serve in the military by executive order of President Lincoln. What say you to this?" Her closing question was short and to the point.

Rob took just a moment to connect her remarks to his current circumstances, particularly that they had found his uniform and orders, yet he arrived dressed as a civilian. They likely thought he was a deserter. He decided not to address that issue right away, and wondered whether they had read and understood his orders and warrants or merely scanned them for such things as his army of allegiance and name. He tried to think of questions he could ask that would reveal the extent of their knowledge about him without giving away anything they did not already possess. He need not have bothered.

"We are aware of your employment with Mr. Pinkerton's agency and a particular relationship you have had with the

United States Army. We also note from the telegraphic messages you carry that you were planning to visit us here. We have no objection to any of this, so long as you agree not to actively carry on any military or other activity of war while you are with us. As best you are able, we ask that you contribute what labor you can to our efforts to sustain the community. It would please us if you would refrain from shaving your face while you are with us. Lastly, we can send a telegraph message to whomever you would like, informing them of your safe arrival and convalescence, should you wish it?"

Sister Elizabeth left nothing to his imagination with this direct revelation. Ending the offer of a telegram as a question clearly left the matter up to Rob. They would tell no one of his presence, if that were his wish. Having no desire to hide from Pinkerton or Molly, he decided to take the sister up on her offer.

"Oh yes, ma'am!" he responded enthusiastically. "If I could get word t' the agency, that would be wonderful!"

He was again surprised when she said, "Good. Then that's settled. There is a telegram addressed to you that we've left un-opened, waiting to learn if you were indeed the Rob Finn on your papers and to whom it is addressed. It arrived at noontime today, before you were recovered. If you'll wait here a moment, I'll fetch it for you." Without further ado, she rose quickly and strode from the room. She was even taller than Rob had originally imagined.  He could recall only rarely  seeing a woman of her height before.

Rob barely had time to mull over in his mind some ideas of what the message might say before the envelope was thrust into his hand and its bearer returned to her seat behind the desk. The look on her face indicated clearly that she was waiting for him to open and read it.  Which he presently did.

The message read:

**No birds in season. Travel possible? Advise.  MF bd AP**

What it meant: No assignments at this time.  Can you travel? (Are you well?)  Reply when able.  Signed, Molly Ferguson by direction of Allan Pinkerton.  This let him know that there was no urgency to his getting back, but that he was looked for.

"They're asking if I kin travel home t' Chicago," Rob offered at the same time reaching to let Sister Elizabeth examine the telegram for herself, which she waved off. "Do you think it's safe for me t' catch a train north in the next day or two?"  While he didn't wish to seem anxious to leave the generous hospitality he had received, he wasn't willing to pretend to any possibility of a religious conversion where none existed.  He was not interested in joining this small sect of avid believers and their unusual practices.

"I'll need to consult our healers, but you should be fine to depart by Friday at the latest.  I doubt we'd recommend you travel by horseback that soon, but riding on the trains shouldn't cause you any problems. I'll let you know. Meanwhile, I'm sure we can arrange to stable your horse while you're away." She again arose and spoke quietly to someone outside her office. She returned once more to her chair and again engaged his eyes with her own. "If you're certain you wouldn't like to stay and learn the deep joy of living peacefully, Mr. Finn, we won't try to dissuade you. As I said earlier, you are free to leave or stay, as you wish."

"Thank ya very kindly, Sister," Rob found it easy to say, "but my employer and my family are expectin' me t' return. I can pay for my time here, an' certainly for boardin' my horse. In fact, I insist on it," he smiled broadly, knowing that the agency would happily cover the expense and it would surely come in handy for this hard-working bunch.

"Your insistence aside, Mr. Finn, our beliefs do not allow us to take payment for basic human hospitality. I can assure you that we appreciate the sentiment, though. And we will be happy to charge a nominal fee for stabling your horse while you are gone, though another arrangement comes to mind." Her intelligent eyes continued to fix him in her gaze.

"An' what might that be?" Rob wondered aloud, his face a mask of puzzlement.

"We couldn't help notice that his size would lend itself to the work of the harness, and we would treat him gently and care for him well. If you consented to let us use him for field and cartage work, we would waive all fees for care and feeding. But we'd need your assurance that he is your beast to hire out." He knew she was referring to the US brand clearly marking Bricks as property of the US government.

"I believe I can give you that assurance within three days of leaving here," Rob was thinking aloud again. "I'm attached to that animal an' want to keep him, an' so was plannin' t' buy him from his present owners. I'll get a bill o' sale an' then wire ya here when that's done. How will that be?" His sincere and winning way brought a smile to her usually staid features. She was quite pretty when she smiled, he noticed.

"That will be satisfactory for our purposes, Mr. Finn. One thing further. You mentioned your employer and family. Are you married, and do you have children?" Again the direct, penetrating eye contact matched the simplicity of the question.

"My wife died in April from the cholera, as did two of our sons," he answered with a note of sadness. He brightened a bit when he added, "But my remainin' two daughters and two sons are healthy, strappin' youngsters!" His pride and joy were evident in his face.

"They would be welcome to visit as well, when you return to collect your horse. We have much to offer a family such as yours."

184 | KEITH R. BAKER

"I thank ya for that, Sister," Rob answered as he considered the idea. "I've no idea yet that we'd take ya up on yer offer, but ya never can tell."

\* \* \* \*

*Thursday afternoon, September 4th, 1862*
*Outside the Common House, Pleasant Hill Shaker Colony, Kentucky*

The next two days fairly flew by.  He would be catching a train on Friday from nearby Nicholasville, and from there north to Lexington, west to Frankfort, LaGrange and on into Louisville.  Though there had been Rebel activity in each of those locales, the Union remained in control of those rails for the most part, so it was deemed safe for him to attempt his return home.  With the slightly cooler evenings as summer's heat lessened, the days were fair and fine.

Rob had written out a message for one of the community's brothers to carry to the telegraph office in Harrodsburg.  Though the town's population was heavily Confederate-leaning, there had not been much trouble with their telegraph wire system thus far.  His coding even was simpler as he had nothing to hide:

**Arrive office Saturday. RF**

While still under the care of Sister Barbara, Rob's wounds healed marvelously and his health returned nearly to what it was before he was wounded. He learned that she was using poultices and hot packs that were heavily loaded with garlic, comfrey, lavender and other herbs that the Shakers grew in their gardens and fields.

He also learned that Sister Barbara was a married woman, having originally joined the Shakers with her husband, some fifteen years before. Her husband had since left to pursue other avenues of life. The couple had had two daughters before the family moved to Pleasant Hill: Rebecca, who was now eighteen and Olivia, who was now sixteen. Their surname was Heinz. Because of the sameness, he inquired as to whether there could be any family connection between them and Jeffery Heinz of St. Louis. Thursday afternoon, the day before his scheduled departure from Pleasant Hill, was when Rob asked about the family name.

"My husband's family is from St. Louis and his younger brother is named Jeffery," Sister Barbara responded. "He is uncle to our daughters. How do you know him?" she wondered.

"We met just a short while ago for the first time," Rob confided. "We had a mutual business interest in St. Louis." This was not strictly true; neither was it an outright lie. He knew he would need to be careful not to reveal too much.

"Well, people say that the world is growing smaller every day, and, what with all the railroads and telegraphs, I suppose that to be true. Should you see him again, it would please me if you would give him our warmest regards. We've not seen him in all the years since we left St. Louis. He was always very good to me and our girls. I suppose John, that's my husband's name, has gone back to St. Louis. That was his plan when he left the community. That was more than five years ago. We've had no word from him since. This life is harder on some people than others," she added. "It is too severe for some men." She looked down and away, and knitted her hands briefly. At that she halted her sharing. She seemed distracted by the memories she was experiencing.

Rob agreed that he would carry her greeting to Jeff the next time he saw him, then took his leave from the woman who had nursed him back to health. He thanked her, for he was sincerely grateful for her care. Not wanting to cause her further painful memories, he stalked off for the men's side of the nearby dormitory building.

That evening, after dinner, Rob was looking for Sister Elizabeth so he could conclude their agreement regarding Bricks, and also to offer his thanks for all he had received from these wonderful and gracious people. He found her in her office in the Common House.

In addition to the details of their agreement about his horse, saddle and tack, Rob surprised the eldress by telling her he did not want the rifle nor the saber returned to him. They were free to sell either or both, or to dispose of them as they saw fit. Sister Elizabeth looked thoughtful for a moment before saying, "We're taught to beat swords into plowshares, Mr. Finn, and have no objection to the taking of game animals with a rifle. That one of yours an accurate device, is it?"

"None greater, in my experience," he replied happily. "You won't be disappointed."

"I'm disappointed you didn't have a chance to stay longer, at least long enough to observe one of our Sabbath celebrations, Mr. Finn," the sister spoke in the clear, soft tones he had come to expect from these Shakers. "Life takes us where it will until we put all in the hands of One greater than us all, you see. We hope you will consider our offer of a longer visit in the near future?" The question was gently put and full of goodwill. Sister Elizabeth gave a rare smile as she asked it.

"Sure, an' it's a temptin' offer I'll not be forgettin', Sister!" Rob again enthused with sincerity. "Once I've looked t' what promises an' obligations I owe, I'll next be lookin' t' see when we could get to Pleasant Hill for a stay. It seems t' be a life of peace, one worth trying for, I'll grant. I cannot thank ya enough for everythin', an' I'll be sendin' you the papers for takin' care of Bricks—next week for sure."

* * * *

*Friday, September 5th, 1862*
*Pleasant Hill Shaker Colony, Kentucky*

Rob felt some sadness while he readied himself to leave early the next day. One of the brothers would drive him up to the station in Nicholasville. They had thoughtfully hitched Bricks to the small wagon so that Rob and his horse could enjoy a final time together before their parting. He would miss these kind, gentle, thoughtful people. Though his time among them had been short, he had thoroughly enjoyed their company and peaceful ways. He didn't think their way of life had much long-term appeal for him, but he respected their choices and their ways. He would never forget them. And though he was certain he would be back to collect Bricks, he didn't know when that would be nor how long he would stay.

As he and Brother Tom climbed up onto the seat of the wagon, Rob found another surprise: The men, women and children of the community had lined up on either side of the roadway leading out the gate. Men and boys were on the east side of the northward route, women and girls were on the west. They all waved cheerily as the wagon bearing their recent guest drove away into the distance.

He had plenty to think about during the trip to catch his train. Brother Tom had almost nothing to say, and Rob was pensive enough not to be seeking conversation.

Considering his route on the rails would take him back into Lexington, he wondered if he might detour for a while in that city. Maybe he should attend to unfinished business between himself, the major, and the quartermaster sergeant. He decided firmly against that course at this time. His wounds were not completely healed and he had a family and a job to return to.

When Brother Tom left him at the station he had with him a simple canvas valise that the community had provided, and a cane. His left leg bothered him enough that Sister Barbara insisted he take it along when leaving her care. He had his Colt Pocket Pistol and boot knife secreted upon his person. He did not expect to need either one, but felt comfortable knowing they were close at hand if a situation arose. His derby hat, much worse for all it had survived in the past ten days, was perched jauntily on his head. After all, he was still as Irish as ever.

# CHAPTER ELEVEN

# Leaving Kentucky

*Late morning, Friday, September 5th, 1862*
*The freight railroad siding just north of Lexington, Kentucky*

As the brakes bled off the excess steam once the train had halted, the billowing clouds of the white stuff partially blocked the cavalry horse depot that lay about one hundred fifty yards east of the siding.  As the clouds of steam dissipated, Rob could clearly see the major and the quartermaster sergeant seated at their duty station, the table in front of the tent where he'd first met them.

He wondered if that twosome had waylaid or tricked or deceived anyone else since he had been in their clutches.  Silly question.  Of course they had.  It was the type of men they were, it was what they would do.  Were they worse as people for trying to advance the cause of the South, merely because they wore the uniforms of the North?  If so, what did that say about him?  Rob wore whichever uniform suited his purpose at the moment: North, South, civilian–what did it matter?

No.  He would leave them alone; he would let bygones be
bygones, as the saying went.  If there were any debt to be settled
he was certain their paths would cross again.  He did not know
for certain about the two attackers that had nearly dealt him his
death.  Had their attack been ordered by one or both of these
men?  Rob would probably never know for sure.

What he did know is that they had deliberately put him
on a horse that was spooked by canon fire and they had given
him a map and directions that would take him into the midst of
the Rebel camps, rather than overlooking them.  Had he not re-
lied on his own wits and experience, he would likely be in a Confederate prison camp right now.  Or worse.  Here were two more
people he would never forget, though he would like to.

The conductor came through the car and announced that
they would be leaving as soon as the engineer and fireman had
seen to loading sufficient water and wood for the trip–he estimated no more than twenty minutes.  Rob decided to stretch his
legs and relieve himself while the opportunity presented itself.  He
left his cane and valise aboard when he climbed down onto the
platform

He hurriedly took care of his business at the side building,
and did what he could not to limp noticeably–he did not want to
become dependent on using a cane.  As he rounded the privy barrier leading away from the men's public relief station, Rob heard
a familiar voice with a nasal southern drawl to it.

"Well, Sergeant, we thought that was you light'n' from th' train. Lose yer stripes, di'ja?" taunted the sweetly wheedling voice of Sergeant Waters.

"An' yer big rifle, too?" joined in the equally syrupy Major Donovan.

The two of them rushed him. Waters was taking his legs out while Donovan swung at his face. Rob's quick reflexive block kept Donovan's knife from carving out his right eye, but did not keep its point from digging painfully into his cheekbone. His left hand retrieved his boot knife by instinct, and that blade was plunged into the chest of his senior assailant. Rob's now-free right hand drew his pistol and fired twice, at point-blank range, into the sergeant's face. As fast as that it was over. Two uniformed men were down, dead or dying. The huge civilian stood over them with blood pumping from the hole in his right cheek. Other than that, and looking stunned, he seemed fine.

"Them two jumped him," called a civilian bystander, "He never had a choice. The big guy was just defending himself."

"That's so," joined a teamster from his seat atop his consignment load. "I seen the whole thing."

"So did I, so did I," added the conductor. "I saw them follow him from the platform over to the relief station when he left the train, so I kept my eye on those two. Never saw anything like that before! You really handled those two. Why'd they want to do that, d'ya suppose?"

"Darned if I know." Rob's words were garbled by the fact that he was holding a handkerchief to his cheek to help stop the considerable blood flow. "I didn't do anything to them."

Because of the gunshots and the proximity to the city, a city policeman arrived shortly. Though all the witnesses' stories matched, the man was not satisfied that something more suspicious hadn't taken place, beyond the killing of two attackers by their intended victim. Rob staunchly denied knowing any reason why these two Union soldiers could want to molest him.

Even after taking written statements from the conductor and willing bystanders, the policeman, Officer Murray, believed it was his duty to investigate further, so he detained Rob. The conductor could not delay the train any longer, and so, with a final attestation that he was witness to Rob's innocence, the man retrieved and returned Rob's valise and cane to him, then boarded the train, which promptly left on its way north.

After the small gathering of witnesses and excited onlookers finally disbursed, Murray turned to Rob and said, "We're going to the nearest precinct house, now, sir, and I'll thank you t' go along peacefully."

Seeing no good alternative to that offer, Rob surrendered his knife and pistol and submitted to being handcuffed, a new experience for him. He again found himself questioning the plans and logic of a so-called "benign deity." None of this made any sense to him.

The processing paperwork at the police station did not take long and Rob was soon being led to a holding cell. He was encouraged by its cleanliness and lack of foul odor. He was given a small tray of food with a cup of water, surprised to discover that it was all of good quality. His spirits, which drooped when he entered the station, began to lift.

It was getting on toward evening when he met the next member of the law profession that would have a say in his future, the precinct's reigning officer. Captain Peter O'Meara was introduced by Murray as Rob was led into his office. Rob was still in handcuffs, though in such a way that they did not trouble him much.

Captain O'Meara looked at Rob, then at the papers on his desk again. When he returned his gaze to Rob, the look there was one Rob could not quite guess at. What was the man thinking? The captain told Officer Murray to remove the handcuffs.

"I'll come right t' the point, Finn. You're big, you can handle yourself in a tight spot. You look like you've been around a bit. You're probably a little old for what I have in mind, but how would you like to do some police work? We're always short-handed around here, and I think you could fit the ticket. Besides all that, you're Irish, and we Irishmen got t' stick together!" He was grinning at his own last remark.

Though greatly relieved to learn he was not under arrest for killing his two attackers, Rob was still in a precarious position. He didn't want to reveal his true position with the Pinkerton Agency and the US Army in case he needed his cover story in this area again. He didn't want to reject the offer out-of-hand, lest he give offense to the ranking lawman in this area, never a good idea. He decided to feel his way along carefully.

"That's mighty nice o' you, Captain. Mind if I ask a few questions o' my own?"

"Go right ahead. Man's got a right to know what he's lettin' himself in for," the captain allowed.

"Well, sir, I'm from Wisconsin, an' no offense intended, but back home, pretty much everyone supports the Union cause. Those that don't, say so. What I'm seeing here is that folks aren't always what they say, if you take my meanin', sir."

"I do take your meanin', an' no offense from it, Finn. You're probably talkin' about the damned KGC, an' yer right–we got more than our share of 'em around here. My man Murray suspects the two that tried t' clobber you are part of that crowd– we try t' keep an eye on what they're up to." The captain paused. "Why, you're not part o' that lot, too, are ya?"

"No sir, not at all," he would reveal some, but not all of his real mission, on faith that the captain was telling the truth. "I'm actually here t' work for the Union against the treasonous organization. More than that, I cannot say. I have my orders." Rob set his jaw firmly, then continued, "I was on my way back t' my headquarters when those two decided to do me in."

"I see how it is, then," Captain O'Meara nodded. "You're already one of us." He grinned widely again, and Rob was further relieved that he would not be pressed for details that he was loathe to provide. "What can we do to help you on your way, Finn?"

"I could use some sleep so I can catch the train tomorrow–if there is one. Nothin' fancy."

"If ya wouldn't be insulted by it, how about ya sleep the night in that cell we had ya in? It's still clean. We'll give you breakfast in the mornin', give ya back yer gun and knife an' send ya on yer way. How does that suit?"

"'Tis better than I was hopin' for, Captain, it suits me fine. Thank you." His weariness was suddenly over him like a blanket, a blanket he couldn't wait to wrap himself to sleep in.

* * * *

*6:30 a.m. Saturday, September 6th, 1862*
*Northwest Precinct Station, Lexington, Kentucky*

Rob woke to the sound of a fork tapping gently on the bars of the cell, Officer Murray with a plate of eggs, bacon and toast, and a steaming cup of coffee. He remembered that the food he'd received the evening before was good; this was even better. He ate with a hearty appetite, though he had to chew more slowly than usual, owing to the wound in his right cheek. It was sore, as was to be expected, but was not overly swollen nor hot to the touch. Rob hoped he could remain free from infection while he traveled home.

Murray sat with Rob while he ate and sipped from his own coffee cup as he watched Rob hungrily devour his plate of food.

"Doesn't look like that cheek is going to bother you too much," suggested the policeman, "but you should probably get it looked at before long." This was offered more in the way of friendly small talk, rather than concern. "Sorry to have dragged you in here for nothin'. Just followin' orders, you understand. I don't have the authority t' make decisions out on the street. You know how that is, right?"

"Sure, sure," answered Rob, "no hard feelings." And it was true. He bore the other man no grudge for taking what action he believed his position demanded of him. Also, this way, he was cleared of any wrongdoing, got a good night's rest and a decent breakfast. There was nothing to be upset about, other than that it was already Saturday morning, so there was no way he would make it to the agency offices in Chicago before Monday.

He hurried to finish breakfast as he was eager to resume his journey north. And he now needed to stop at a telegraph office to notify Pinkerton of his delay. When he asked where the nearest wire office was located, he was again treated to the hospitality of this police precinct.

"We've got a key right here in the precinct, Finn. What d'ya want t' send?"

Rob wrote the agency's key address and the message:

### Delayed. Monday a.m. RF

... and left the building as soon as he received confirmation that it was sent.

# CHAPTER TWELVE

# Planning Ahead

*Sunday, September 7th, 1862*
*Chicago, Illinois*

His return to Chicago was not as swift nor smooth as he had hoped. As was becoming so common with the war effort, train delays and interrupted service added many hours to even routine trips. Nevertheless, it was uneventful. He was able to sleep a good deal during the long stretches of track between cities. He did not get down from the train in Chicago until Sunday afternoon, however.

When he arrived at his usual sleeping room, (which the agency provided in a private home), he decided to get a bath before dinner. As he soaked in the bathtub, Rob examined his right shoulder and bicep and then his left thigh. (He had been directed by Sister Barbara to keep his wounds and stitches out of water for another seven or eight days.) The condition of the healing, how complete and solid was the healthy scarring, was almost unbelievable. Those Shakers must really know their herbal medicines!

He finished his quick soak and then hopped out of the tub. He couldn't see his cheek to observe that wound without a mir-

202 | KEITH R. BAKER

ror, which he did not have at the moment. It was tender to the touch, yet remained without swelling or heat. From the reactions of others he'd passed since the incident occurred, he knew that it presented quite a sight.

He exited the public bath in the rear of the barber shop, feeling much better, and having already put on clean clothes, Rob went to dinner. He had thought about visiting Molly at her home, and nearly did so. In the end though, he decided it best not to intrude unannounced, especially looking frightful. Tomorrow would be soon enough to renew their friendship.

Before turning in for the night, he carefully dabbed at his cheek wound with a clean white handkerchief and was relieved when it came away clean. His sleep was peaceful and deep, with the exception of one dream episode when he re-lived the two men attacking him in the woods. He awoke with a start, swinging left and right to protect himself. He remained awake for a moment longer, realizing that he had twice been attacked by two men on this mission, and both times he was the only one to walk away with his life.

\* \* \* \*

*8:00 a.m. Monday, September 8th, 1862*
*Pinkerton Agency Offices, Chicago, Illinois*

With all the extra rest he had had on Saturday and Sunday, Rob woke earlier than usual, got himself ready, dressed, and ate breakfast before arriving at the office an hour before the 8:00 a.m. opening time. He had not shaved since the morning he left Richmond on his way south over two weeks earlier. His beard was starting to fill in and thus offered a little cover for the lower portion of the wound on his cheek. From just below the eye to the line of the beard was a very noticeable cut that was still ragged and raw.

When Molly came through the door at 7:30 and saw him standing by the counter, she put her hand to her mouth and gasped, "Oh, Rob! What in the world happened to you?!" Hers was not the only such expression of concern he heard from co-workers that day, but it was the most heartfelt and most welcome among them.

Allan Pinkerton was also returning from an out-of-town trip and was later than usual getting into the office. As soon as he arrived, he summoned Rob to join him in his private office to render his verbal report on his mission. The door was closed after Rob entered the room, as usual.

Rob was seated on the couch in the office. After giving his report, Pinkerton asked him to stand and remove his jacket, vest and shirt, which Rob did. Pinkerton asked him if he would mind removing his small shirt, which Rob also did. Pinkerton got up from behind the desk and came around to where Rob was now standing and examined his right chest, shoulder and arm without touching him. Again there was the characteristic low whistle that the spy master gave out when impressed by something. The suturing was very even, small and tight. Yet there was no puckering of the skin captured within the cat-gut stitching.

"This is the worst of yer three injuries, Rob?" he asked. He had already given the facial wound close scrutiny before they sat down.

"'Tis that, sir. Sister Barbara seemed t' think th' stabbing t' my leg could cause a limp later on, but said it was healing fine. I've decided not t' shave my beard until my cheek's done healing."

"I think ya should keep the beard, Rob, but for right now, we need t' have ya see a specialist about yer cheek. It won't do for ya t' have a big scar makin' ya easier t' mark an' remember. Not in our line o' work, lad."

Rob got himself dressed again, and he and Pinkerton left the office and headed north. During their short trek, Pinkerton brought up the outcome of Rob's latest mission.

"Rob, I know ya did yer best t' remove the target ya were sent for; ya must believe that. Ya must also have read the newspaper reports about Kirby Smith's complete victory at Richmond?" Pinkerton began the conversation benignly enough. Rob didn't know where this was going, so merely nodded that, yes, he had seen the reports.

"Well, the point here, Rob, is just how important t' the Union cause are our efforts, and how easy it is for bad information t' cause our missions t' fail. If we had known the real where-about of Smith earlier, ya could have been sent out that much sooner with a better chance of success. Do ya see the value of having good operatives and detectives in the field, lad?" As he continued, Pinkerton warmed to his subject to the point of being fairly passionate by the time he posed his last question.

"Oh, yes, sir, I do!" came Rob's emphatic reply. "Good intelligence makes all the difference!" His actual enthusiasm for the topic was probably not quite as great as his voice implied, but he saw no reason to disappoint the man who had consistently supported him.

"That's what I was hopin' t' hear ya say, Rob. After today's visit to the surgeon, and y've had a little while t' heal, I'll be wantin' ya t' head up our intelligence office in St. Louis. What-d'ya think o' that, lad?" Once again the normally stoic Scotsman surprised Rob with a broad grin.

"Well, I ... I don't know what t' say, sir!" Rob beamed back at his patron. And there was no lie in those words, either.

"So we won't be needing yer long-range talents again, though I will always think of ya as Longshot. Do ya mind if I call ya that from time-to-time, Rob?"

"No, sir. Being called by a name is no hardship." This again was a truthful reply.

206 | KEITH R. BAKER

"Good, good," agreed Pinkerton. "Still, it's a shame the Sharps rifle was ruined by yer attackers." Rob's conscience barely registered any guilt at having lied to his boss about the gun.

They continued on for another couple of blocks, then entered a tall masonry building with a dressed-stone front. On the third floor, they entered the spaces occupied by Dr. Walter Knock, whose specialty, appearing neatly lettered under his name on the glass of the door, read "Surgical Remedies of Every Sort." Once inside, Pinkerton announced himself and his purpose to the receptionist, who recognized the agency owner at once.

"Yes, sir, Mr. Pinkerton," acknowledged the smart-looking young lady, "Let me see if Doctor Knock can fit you in this morning's schedule."

She disappeared down a narrow hallway leading to other rooms with closed doors and entered one of them after knocking twice. When she returned, she was followed by a short, balding, bespectacled man who Rob guessed to be in his sixties. The doctor waved them through with a kindly smile and friendly greeting of "Good morning, gentlemen, good morning." His accent identified him as German-born.

When the three men were gathered in one of the examining rooms with the door closed, Allan Pinkerton proceeded to share his concern that the cut on Rob's cheek be attended to immediately before scar tissue became a problem.

"Ah. Umm, hmm. Yes. Yes. I see vot it is dat has you concerned, Mr. Pinkerton. I agree vit' you. Dis needs to be taken care of at once. I vill be able to get started in about one hour. Leave the patient vit' me, und he vill be ready dis afternoon."

Rob had seen the cut in the mirror at his room again this morning before leaving for the office. The edges were rough and jagged, with several areas that protruded above the level of the surrounding skin. He had just assumed he would have a wide, lumpy scar when the healing was completed. The thought did not bother him particularly until Pinkerton pointed out that it would be a permanent identifying mark—a detriment in the spying business.

After a half-hour wait with a copy of the last Saturday's Harper's Weekly, in which he had been reading an article about the iron-clad steam frigate named Ironsides, the receptionist came into the room where he'd been examined by the doctor and led Rob across the hall to a larger room with tall windows on two walls. He was asked to remove the clothing from his upper body and be seated in a chair that reminded him of a barber's chair. She then handed him a white linen cloth that she had taken from a paper wrapping, and helped him use it to drape his torso. The doctor entered the room before Rob was completely covered and stopped the process.

"Young man, let me look at dat shoulder und arm," the old physician ordered. He then changed eyeglasses, put a small reflective disk on his head and focused its beam of reflected light on to Rob's wounds while he examined them briefly. "Excellent. Excellent. How long ago did dis happen?" asked Doctor Knock.

The balance of his time within the doctor's surgery consisted of similar questions, with Rob answering as best he could. This was followed by tilting him back in the chair, being draped with the cloth earlier unwrapped and being anesthetized with chloroform. He remembered nothing of the procedure, but when he regained consciousness and was shown his face in a mirror, he could see that he had been tended to by a master. All raggedness was gone from the cut in his cheek, as were the bumps and roughness. The edges were sewn together with the tiniest of stitches imaginable along the thinnest possible line separating them. Though there was soreness present, it was nothing compared to what he had already been through.

The good doctor and his staff allowed Rob some additional time to recover, during which he was again reading the September 6th, 1862 edition of Harper's Weekly. So engrossing did he find the article titled, "The President and Slavery," that he determined to purchase a copy of the publication from a newsstand along the street. What he had found most disturbing was the President's declaration that "his sole exclusive aim is to restore the Union, without reference to slavery." It sounded as if Jeffery Heinz's perspective on the issues underlying this terrible war were correct, a thought that grew more troubling every time Rob bumped into it.

He was in the waiting area, as he'd been instructed, when Allan Pinkerton returned to claim him. The receptionist explained the proper care of his newly-sutured cheek, mentioning that the doctor also had removed the stitches from his shoulder, arm, and leg while he was under the chloroform. She then handed him a small reminder card with an appointment date and time for September 15th, one week later. They would then re-examine all of his wounds and remove the stitches from his cheek, assuming all was well.

On the walk back to the agency, Rob did indeed purchase a copy of the Harper's Weekly edition that had captured his attention. Pinkerton suggested that, after taking care of some small administrative matters at the office, Rob should take the balance of the week off to recover and visit his family again in Darien. He should return to that agency on the following Monday, the same day as his next doctor's appointment.

"There's one more thing I've thought t' talk t' ya about, Rob," Pinkerton began hesitantly, "that bein' the matter of you and Molly Ferguson. I don't approve of office romances, as ya know. With yer family losses an' John being killed in the line o'duty, I decided t' overlook some things. Ya both needed t' mend. Now, I'm not so sure it's a good idea. I'm not sayin' ya absolutely can't see her anymore, though I think that would be best.

But ya must be completely detached from each other at the office. I've already spoken t' her about it."

It had been the furthest thing from Rob's mind, and so he found the pronouncement startling. He thought about it some before they reached the offices and decided it made sense. They could not, should not, carry on like moon-struck teenagers if they were to work in a professional environment together.

He had been thinking of inviting Molly for another visit to Darien while he would be there during the next week. Pinkerton's restatement of the agency's policy about such things caused him to change his mind. He'd have some more thinking to do while he was at home. His recent mission, with his two near-brushes with death had been weighing on his mind some. Rob needed to sort through his priorities regarding his family, his marital status, his work and his part in this war. So he need be in no rush to settle things with Molly, or anyone else, for that matter.

When they entered the offices again, Molly did not even look up from her desk. Rob could see from the movement of her eyes that she was taking in every move that he and Pinkerton made. She did a good job of keeping her observational activity to herself.

Since it was early afternoon, he figured he could catch a train north and be at home before midnight, much earlier if the change of trains in Racine went well. He was determined to try.

As he prepared to take his leave from Allan Pinkerton, he brought up a subject that had been bothering him, that being his fifty-dollar debt of gold. He had been intending to pay it back, in full, before this time. He had put aside forty dollars toward what he owed, and hoped to add the remaining sum of ten dollars presently, so that he could pay it back to Pinkerton upon his return the following Monday. He expressed his plan to Pinkerton, who, as usual, looked at him intensely and unblinkingly from his desk chair.

"I appreciate yer concern, Rob, really I do," started the Scot, "but considering all y've done for this agency, an' all y've sacrificed, I'd already decided t' forgive that debt. Consider it paid in full." When Rob started to object, Pinkerton interjected flatly, "There'll be no more discussion, Rob. My mind's made up. Enjoy yer time with yer family, lad."

Rob thanked his employer profusely for his generosity. He could not believe his good fortune. Before he turned to leave, though, Pinkerton tacked on a final thought, "We'll look forward t' seein' ya next Monday, Rob. Don't forget where ya work. Yer next assignment will be startin' shortly in St. Louis, an' looks to be going westward from there." Both men smiled, and then Rob nodded, turned on his heel and left. He tried not to notice Molly's gaze following him as he exited the agency's outer door.

\* \* \* \*

His train was on time leaving Chicago and arriving in Racine, and his connection with the westbound line went better than he could ever remember. They pulled into the Darien station at 6:45 pm, several hours earlier than Rob thought even possible. Even though his travel time was so much less, he had had plenty of time to think of what he would say to his children and Maggie about his latest work, and about his upcoming assignment, which already sounded as if it would take him from home much longer than any of his previous jobs for Pink.

There had been no time for purchasing gifts, but his recent windfall of not having to repay the fifty-dollar loan meant that he would be able to be generous with his family and housekeeper—a generosity he planned to share the very next day.

These and other thoughts occupied his mind as he strolled along in the cool September evening air. He was remembering that it was just about a year before that he and Bridget had strolled along this same street, on a similar lovely evening. Neither of them could have imagined the losses and hardships which lay ahead of them. They had been happy and full of life, even as he prepared to depart for his first duty as an enlisted man in the Army of the United States.

Several of the townspeople, including Thomas Duffy, had encouraged and enabled his enlistment as sergeant for their local company, The State Line Rifles. Rob was seen as being capable and mature, someone who would look after the town's young men who were going off to fight this noble war. Duffy's connections with William Penn Lyons, who had been appointed a captaincy, and also his friendship with then-Governor Louis Harvey, had assured Rob's non-commissioned officer role. But what none of them predicted was his uncanny long-range ability with the rifle, and his speed and strength in close-quarters battle–the two things that most brought him to Pinkerton's attention.

Now, a year later, Bridget was no longer. He could hardly believe she'd been gone five months; he really couldn't even believe she was gone at all. And Michael and Henry, too! When he stopped to think about it, it was all too much. And yet, life had gone on.

He determined that he would finally seek out the county's sanitation commissioners this week and learn exactly where his sons had been buried. If necessary he would use some of his "found" money to have them properly buried next to their mother. He would visit and decorate Bridget's grave–he would pay the parish church to say masses in their names. There were lots of details he would attend to while home for this week. The most important of those was attending to his surviving family.

Rob's left leg felt fine, so he carried his cane hooked into the crook of his arm.

He was planning to again knock softly when he arrived so as not to startle anyone. As he stepped forward on the porch to rap on the door, it swung inward and both Cath and Maggie swarmed him. Maggie had happened to be looking out the window and there was just enough light left for her to catch his unmistakeable silhouette as he approached the house.

The family's collective joy filled the main room of the small house as Rob picked up and hugged each one in turn, including Maggie. All their emotions were running high and tears mixed with laughter were obvious all around. The women and children were alarmed by the pink wound on the big man's cheek. Despite the fact that it had been expertly repaired, it was quite visible up close. Because of their reaction to the least of his wounds and his cane, he thought it best not to share the worst of his injuries with them at this time.

The three youngest children were put to bed for the night while Rob sat up with Cath and Maggie. Even though he had been away for exactly a month, it seemed to him that both of these girls had again blossomed. He could no longer consider them girls, they were both young women. Cath's thirteen birthday had passed while he was away. He was planning on treating the entire family to a dinner outing at the town's one hotel restaurant, complete with a stop at the ice cream parlor afterwards. This would be to celebrate Cath's birthday, though a little belatedly.

Both the women were nodding their agreement, all smiles and rosy-cheeked until Cath stopped and took on a serious look.

"Daddy," she began, turning to Rob, "I have a favor t' ask." She looked so grave compared to a moment before, that he worried something might be wrong. "Could everyone please call me Catherine?"

Rob's instantaneous relief showed through in his outburst of laughter. "Is that all, me darlin'? Ya bet we'll call ya Catherine!" She blushed a little at his response, then shushed her father against waking the younger children.

The next evening, an elaborate meal in Darien's hotel restaurant was enjoyed by each member of their party, from the youngest to the oldest. But the stop at the ice cream parlor afterwards brought more smiles and delight than Rob could have imagined.

He knew the remainder of their week together would race past quickly, far too quickly for his liking. For right now, however, he put that out of his mind, refusing to let it spoil their days together. Rob Finn counted himself a truly fortunate man, with much to be thankful for.

## The End

You've finished this first book in the LONGSHOT series, and it is my sincere hope that you've enjoyed the story and the writing. I've worked hard at it and had a lot of help. As it happens, much that's in the book is real, including some of the characters. Four decades of avid genealogical and historical research have provided a good stockpile to draw on, and there's plenty more in the heap.

Rob, Maggie, Catherine, Molly, Allan Pinkerton, Bricks, and others survive into the next book; some even make it into the volume after that.

The next title in the series is: LONGSHOT INTO THE WEST. It picks up very shortly after LONGSHOT IN MISSOURI ended, with Rob and company being sent out to the western territories that were not yet part of the States, when it was still quite wild. I hope you'll come along for the ride.

Thank you for reading Longshot In Missouri. It is my sincere hope you found it an enjoyable story. If so, there are a couple of things, I'd like you to consider. The first would be to share your impressions with your reading friends and family. The second is to offer your honest review at www.Amazon.com. These two things are what keep writers writing.

Lastly, should you be interested, go to my website: www.KeithRBaker.com and sign up for the newsletter. I promise not to bombard you with announcements. But you will be notified of FREE items, as well as Giveaways and similar promotions. It only takes a moment. Some of the FREE items are books or short stories. Of those, some will only be available to subscribers–so it is to your benefit to do so. And please do not hesitate to share with your friends and family.

Thanks again for reading my work–I really appreciate it. Without you it would all be pointless.

Books by Keith R. Baker:

Fiction:  The Longshot series

Longshot In Missouri

Longshot Into The West


Non-fiction:

The Beginner's Guide To Your First Handgun

ABOUT THE AUTHOR

In addition to being an avid history and genealogy buff, Keith has been an active outdoorsman his entire life. He has worn a variety of hats in the business world and completed two periods of duty with the US Navy. His hobbies apart from reading and research include shooting, teaching others the basics of gun safety & handling. Keith sometimes takes an active role in local and regional politics as a public speaker and campaign consultant.

Keith and his wife Leni have enjoyed living several places in the US, including Illinois, Wisconsin, Missouri and Montana. They have two adult children, two adult foster children and nine grandchildren scattered around the country.

# END NOTES

It is always the intent of this author to weave together real, actual historical events, places, and persons together with the fictional characters, happenings, and conversations that can improve our understanding and appreciation of how humankind have arrived in our current condition.

To that end, let me give just a few of the real historical facts contained in LONGSHOT IN MISSOURI for you to research further, should such be your interest.

**The SHARPS Rifle** that Rob uses is a real gun–a veritable instrument of precision and accuracy. Though the long shot he makes with it in the opening paragraph of the book is extra-ordinary, it is not impossible. Rob, a.k.a. Longshot, is an extra-ordinary man–not an impossible one.

**Pleasant Hill Shaker Community** in Kentucky is very real. You can still visit to get a feel for life in the 19th century and even get a wonderful Sunday breakfast/brunch there during many months of the year. Don't take my word for it; visit yourself. Look for it with a Google Search.

The battle of **Richmond, Kentucky** was a huge victory for the Confederacy and an even bigger defeat for the North. General Kirby Smith was brilliant. Some historians

222 | KEITH R. BAKER

believe that, had it not been for the overwhelming Southern victory, the war might have ended as much as two years sooner. At the same time, a more successful follow-up by the CSA might even have reversed the outcome of that war.

The **Knights of the Golden Circle (KGC)** were a real secret society who supported the Confederate position in the Civil War. Some say they continue to exist. There's lots to look at on this subject if you are willing to find it.

**Camp Douglas, Chicago**, was not only a real place, its record of atrocities and criminal negligence far surpass anything that was done at Andersonville. Again, don't take my word for it. Keep in mind that the victors write the history books that are used in schools. The victors also always prosecute some among the defeated–whether or not such prosecution is warranted.

**Harper's Weekly**, particularly the Saturday, September 6th, 1862 edition referred to on page 227 really does contain an article titled, "The President and Slavery". If you received a public school education in the Northern States, or if you taught in that setting, you really owe it to yourself to read the article. You can probably guess how to find it ...

~ Keith

Printed in Great Britain
by Amazon

33959152R00139